DRACULA'S AMERICA

SHADOWS OF THE WEST

HUNTING GROUNDS

Jonathan Haythornthwaite

OSPREY GAMES

Osprey Games, an imprint of Osprey Publishing Ltd
c/o Bloomsbury Publishing Plc
PO Box 883, Oxford, OX1 9PL, UK
Or
c/o Bloomsbury Publishing Inc.
1385 Broadway, 5th Floor, New York, NY 10018
E-mail: info@ospreypublishing.com

www.ospreygames.co.uk

OSPREY and OSPREY GAMES are trademarks of Osprey
Publishing Ltd, a division of Bloomsbury Publishing Plc.

First published in Great Britain in 2018

A CIP catalogue record for this book is available from the
British Library.

Jonathan Haythornthwaite has asserted his right under the
Copyright, Designs, and Patents Act, 1988, to be identified as
the author of this book.

ISBN: PB: 9781472826534
ePub: 9781472826541
ePDF: 9781472826558
XML: 9781472826565

18 19 20 21 22   10 9 8 7 6 5 4 3 2 1

Typeset in Adobe Garamond and Alternate Gothic
Printed in China through [XXXX]

Osprey Publishing supports the Woodland Trust, the UK's
leading woodland conservation charity. Between 2014 and 2018
our donations are being spent on their Centenary Woods
project in the UK.

All the artwork in this book was produced by RU-MOR, a
freelance illustrator and miniature sculptor. She was born in
Tarragona, Spain, and studied Fine Arts at the University of
Seville, specializing and working on artwork restoration. She
began her professional career in 2000, sculpting historical,
fantasy, and science-fiction miniatures, and has since provided
illustrations for various Spanish RPGs, books, and card games.

All the photos in this book were kindly provided by Nick Eyre
and Kevin Dallimore of North Star Military Figures (www.
northstarfigures.com), and show figures from North Star's
official *Dracula's America* range, sculpted by Mike Owen and
Mark Copplestone, and from Artizan Designs' Wild West line
(www.artizandesigns.com).

CONTENTS

INTRODUCTION

Welcome to *Hunting Grounds*, the first supplement for the *Dracula's America* Gothic Western skirmish game!

These books will contain a whole heap of new material for you to include in your existing games and campaigns – *Hunting Grounds* contains two new Factions and optional Skinwalker Tribal Themes, new Hired Guns, Weapons (including Close Combat weapons!), Gear, Arcane Powers, and a brand new Bestiary of NPCs from the spirit world.

As always, the bulk of these additions are entirely modular and compatible with the *Dracula's America: Shadows of the West* rulebook – so feel free to use the new material you like and leave out the rest – they'll slot right in alongside the core rules!

As you will hopefully have realised by now, playing *Dracula's America* is first and foremost about having fun telling great stories on the table-top – these expansions will take this to the next level by including new linked scenarios that you can play in one-off games, or follow from start to finish as a narrative campaign.

But that's not all – those of you with even more ambition can take part in an ongoing story arc that will run throughout the series – an over-arching storyline that will expand with each book, and see your Posse travel to some of the darkest corners of Dracula's America...

The West is about to get a whole lot weirder, my friends, and I sincerely hope you enjoy the ride!

Jonathan Haythornthwaite

THE SETTING

Welcome to Indian Territory

The area known as 'Indian Territory' encompasses a wide region – much of which has traditionally been sacred land to the Native American tribes who call it home.

The Treaty of Laramie had been in effect since before the Civil War and the rise of Dracula – the tribes kept to their territory, and the US Government laid claim to the surrounding areas. As long as the tribes were left in peace, they would keep to their land and never trouble the Government.

At least, that was the theory...

THE BLACK HILLS

A sacred land to the Sioux who dwell within the Indian Territory, the Black Hills are technically 'off-limits' to non-Native American peoples.

Unfortunately, the Black Hills also hide abundant natural resources – George Custer's Black Hills Expedition discovered gold in the region. Though technically in violation of the Treaty of Laramie, and therefore illegal, this fact was conveniently ignored by Dracula's resource-starved government struggling to rebuild in the wake of the Civil War, and by the hordes of desperate prospectors that flooded the area hoping to make their fortune.

The Native American retribution for these transgressions was often swift and brutal, but rather than driving the greedy hordes away it merely invited equally brutal reprisals as newspapers printed increasingly lurid tales of these 'unprovoked' attacks.

With the discovery of the valuable Arcane fundament known as 'Animus', this tense situation became a powder-keg, ready to explode into violence with the smallest of sparks...

OPPOSITE The Shadow Dragon Tong: Animus Dealer

CONVERGENCE

Their sacred lands invaded and their treaty with the US Government up in flames, the Sioux could only watch in horror as their territory was violated by greedy prospectors.

White Raven, spiritual leader of the Skinwalker Tribes and a Lakota Sioux himself, desperately sought a refuge for his people. He found it, in the other realm known to the Native American peoples as the Hunting Grounds.

This realm of spirits could be reached via temporary 'doors' known as Convergence, found where the Hunting Grounds overlapped with the physical world. From here, the Skinwalker Tribes could start a new life away from the teeming hordes, regroup, and perhaps even strike out at the hated railroads from unexpected directions. It was perfect...

However, something went awry with White Raven's ritual and he found he could not reliably control the number, location, or duration of Convergences – in some places, the Hunting Grounds were irrevocably meshed with our own plane, allowing creatures to freely pass from one to the other (often unknowingly).

It was into one of these 'doorways' that a desperate gold prospector known as Zeke Matheson stumbled, one fateful day in late 1875 and made a discovery that would change his life – and the fate of the entire Indian Territory – forever...

DEADWOOD CITY

Squatting precariously within the bounds of Indian Territory, Deadwood started life as a small mining town during the original gold rush in the Black Hills.

With the discovery of Convergences and Animus, a new wave of settlers heading West to seek a better life saw Deadwood's population explode out of all proportion as the town swiftly became the thriving hub of the lucrative Animus trade.

The brand new rail artery, known as the Deadwood Line, now carries Animus to wealthy buyers back East, and the independent mining settlement has quickly become a sprawling boomtown whose inhabitants are proud to call Deadwood City.

Yet for all its excitement and allure, Deadwood City is controlled by shadowy forces who vie for power within its dark underbelly of illegal Animus dens, bawdy-houses, and killers-for-hire...

THE HUNTING GROUNDS

'The Hunting Grounds' is in fact the name given by the Native American peoples to the spirit realm – that ethereal plane of existence which runs parallel to our own physical realm.

Other cultures and traditions have their own names for this gloomy place – Purgatory, Hades, Valhalla – to some, it is a 'stopping-off' point on a soul's journey to its ultimate reward in the afterlife. To others, it is the final destination. The ethereal nature of the spirit realm means that it is all of these things – and more...

The spirit and physical realms coexist alongside each other within the cosmic balance of Nature, and each plays as vital a role in the natural order of things as the other. The spirit realm can be imagined as a 'mirror' of the physical – places and people simultaneously exist in both, though their incarnation within the Hunting Grounds is often subtly twisted – those who have walked the twilight trails liken it to looking at objects as if from underwater, or through a desert heat-haze.

Occasionally, the two realms overlap in places where the dimensional 'walls' that separate them are weakest. These Convergences – as they are known to those with knowledge of such things – allow the two worlds to interact, and are the source of many a campfire ghost story!

When a mortal creature dies, its spirit departs this plane and fades into the Hunting Grounds, where it assumes the form most pleasing to it whilst it was alive. For most folks, this is a spectral version of its old physical body and it will retain whatever knowledge and personality it possessed while alive, often re-enacting past glories and reliving old horrors – some unfortunate souls even seem unaware of the fact that they are already dead! Some, however, may reveal their inner corruption upon assuming spirit form – becoming monstrous spirit creatures, such as the bestial Manitou.

The Hunting Grounds, and all the spirits that dwell there, are formed of ethereal energy known as Animus that manifests in concentrated clouds of ectoplasm deep within the Hunting Grounds. This substance is highly sought-after by the many popular spiritualists who ply their trade across America (and indeed, the world), as well as less savoury dabblers in the Arcane arts – for it is rumoured that this 'spirit energy' can be used to empower spells and incantations of all kinds to a dangerous degree.

To most ignorant people however, the Hunting Grounds and the untapped energies they contain are nothing more than ghost stories or theological mysteries that they will unfortunately only get to experience when their time on this mortal coil is up...

ANIMUS

The Arcane fundament known as Animus is concentrated spirit-energy, or ectoplasm. It is a hitherto-untapped source of great (though unpredictable) Arcane energy found only within the Hunting Grounds.

Well-to-do Arcanists back East will pay handsomely for even the merest portion of this amazing substance, since it augments a user's own Arcane power and even unlocks previously dormant powers! Despite the occasional spectacular accident, the demand for more Animus in such rarefied scholarly circles increases with each month. If this was the only effect of the stuff, it would be a potent enough force. However, the substance's effect upon those mortals with no Arcane sensitivity has seen its worth increase twofold!

Distilled Animus acts as a powerful and wholly intoxicating opiate upon the ordinary human mind – sending the hapless user into a dreamlike state of heightened perceptions and waking visions in which they are rendered utterly insensitive to all pain, doubt, and fear. Considering the living nightmare that is existence within Dracula's America, it is small wonder that there are many who would seek solace in the embrace of Animus...

Needless to say, where there is demand there are always those willing to supply – at least, for as long as they can turn a profit from the weakness and suffering of others! At first, the discovery of Convergence saw thousands of desperate, independent 'prospectors' rush to Indian Territory in search of their fortune, driven by tales of men and women striking it rich in the Hunting Grounds over the course of a single day.

Naturally, the Powers That Be were quick to pick up on the opportunities offered by this amazing new resource – Dracula was, of course, concerned that the discovery might mean a shift in the balance of power if a large enough quantity of Animus were to end up in the hands of his rivals. To this end, it wasn't long before the Government clamped down – hard – on unsanctioned prospecting, and an 'Animus tax' was levied against those prospectors who could afford to pay the exorbitant fee to attain the appropriate licence.

As Animus flows out of Indian Territory to satisfy the clamouring masses back East, it must pass through Deadwood City via the now-famous 'Deadwood Line'. This naturally means that Edward Crowley and his Crossroads Cult control the supply. A fact that Crowley uses to effectively extort the Government – the Grand Magister playing a deadly game of veiled threat and counter-threat with Dracula; the two wicked beings circling each other like hungry wolves, each constantly testing the other's strength of will.

And yet, a new power watches these two alpha predators from the illicit Animus dens hidden down the dark alleys of Deadwood – a power brought here by Crowley himself – the Shadow Dragon Tong.

Originally seen as cheap labour to speed along the construction of the Deadwood Line at an incredible rate, the Chinese immigrant workers brought with them this most mysterious criminal organization – seemingly innocent men and women who harboured powers over the spirit realm, and even some who could no longer be truly counted amongst the living!

Desperate to complete his railway, Crowley agreed to cede control of half of Deadwood (the poorer half, naturally!) to the Shadow Dragons, and furthermore not to interfere with the Tong's various 'enterprises' within their territory. It was not long before a black market in illegal Animus was thriving in the dark underbelly of Deadwood – with the Tong's wealth and influence growing accordingly.

Crowley's deal with the leader of the Tong – the shadowy figure known only as Yanluo – may yet prove to be his undoing, for in his greed for the Animus that he hopes will accelerate his Great Ritual, the Grand Magister was perhaps less cautious than he should have been. For one accustomed to sealing unspeakable pacts with the diabolical denizens of the Abyss, Yanluo may well be one devil with whom he should not have dealt!

NEW GAME RULES

The Hunting Grounds

ENTERING THE HUNTING GROUNDS

You may decide that any Game is to take place within the area of a Convergence, where the barriers between the physical and spirit realms are at their weakest. The following rules will then apply.

All models must start the game outside the Hunting Grounds in the physical realm, unless otherwise stated by a Scenario or other special rule.

- Any model that Activates on a red card (Diamonds or Hearts) may declare they are moving into or out of the Hunting Grounds at the start of that Activation – this is free, and does not use up an Action!
- A Spirit-Walker (page 49) may enter or exit the Hunting Grounds at the start or end of any Activation as described above and regardless of the card used. However, they cannot do both in the same Activation. In addition, they may take one other friendly model (mounted models count as a single model) that is in Contact with them along for the ride if you wish.

OPPOSITE Hired Gun: Medium

Whenever a model leaves the Hunting Grounds, roll a D6: on a roll of 1, a Spirit Creature NPC has followed them through into the physical realm – immediately roll on the Spirit Creature table (page 17) to see what it is, then place it D6+1" away from the model in a random direction – as always, use common sense when placing the Creature!

Bottle Checks can be made by eligible models in either realm and the results will affect friendly models in **both** realms.

Unexpected Events can only affect models in the physical realm.

SPIRIT TOKENS

While within the Hunting Grounds, a model or other game element receives a **Spirit Token** (such as a coloured glass bead) to show they are no longer in the physical realm.

A model with a Spirit Token cannot usually affect models without a Spirit Token in any way – they do not block their movement, LOS, and cannot attack them. The reverse is also true.

Furthermore, a model with a Spirit Token can only interact with other game elements that are designated as also being within the Hunting Grounds. This means they are not affected by rough terrain and can freely pass through solid objects, but cannot climb a wall or use stairs that exist in the physical realm, and cannot control Objectives or pick up Loot unless these elements exist in the Hunting Grounds.

This means you need to be careful about when you shift between realms – for example, if your model is standing on the second floor of a building in the physical realm and shifts into the Hunting Grounds, they will immediately drop 'through' the floor and so will count as falling – if in doubt as to what happens, talk it through briefly with the other players and apply a little logic!

Finally, a model with a Spirit Token can never leave the table, even in Scenarios that allow for this.

> A model can never end a Move 'inside' solid terrain or another model.
> Although technically possible, it's simpler (and far less messy!) to disallow this in the interests of gameplay

LOST IN THE HUNTING GROUNDS!

In a Campaign, models that fall as Casualties or Bottle Out while they are within the Hunting Grounds run the risk of being lost within this dismal realm. Put such unfortunate models off to one side, separate from your other Casualties.

After rolling for Injury (if applicable), these models must score a Success on 1 Grit Die or miss the rest of this Campaign Phase.

If successful, they immediately return to the physical realm as described above. On a maximum possible score (e.g. 8 on a D8) they also immediately gain +1 EXP from their experiences in the Hunting Grounds.

SUMMONING IN THE HUNTING GROUNDS (OPTIONAL RULE)

The dimensional walls of the Hunting Grounds are thinner than those of the physical realm and are easily breached by the diabolical denizens of the Abyss. Summoning Entities is therefore a much more risky proposition within the spirit realm, with an increased chance of angry, rogue demons clawing their way from the Abyssal plane!

When a model attempts to Cast the Summon Arcane Power within the Hunting Grounds and fails, then they will accidentally Summon an Abyssal Entity of the Grit Rank, 3" away from them in a random direction – with the appropriate rules below – instead of the intended Summoned Creature.

Abyssal Entities Summoned in this way are 'rogue', and are NPCs in every respect!

For example, a Novice Arcanist declares they will attempt to Summon a Minor Entity while within the Hunting Grounds and fails; and so mistakenly Summons an NPC Fiend!

Lesser Abyssal Entity

	Base Size	Move	Grit	Special
HELLHOUND	25mm	6"	D6	Lesser Entity. Fearsome. A new Unique Summoning for the Crossroads Cult.

Minor Abyssal Entity

	Base Size	Move	Grit	Special
FIEND	25mm	4"	D8	Minor Entity. Flying. Fearsome.

Major Abyssal Entity

	Base Size	Move	Grit	Special
BEHEMOTH	40mm	4"	D10	Major Entity. Flying. Fearsome. Has a breath-attack which uses a 4" Fire Corridor – it will always use this attack if it can catch two or more enemies within the flames – otherwise it acts like a normal NPC.

The Perils of Power

As we have already seen, successfully Casting Arcane Powers while within an area saturated by Animus leaking through from the Hunting Grounds can be a risky proposition – malevolent Entities are uncontrollably drawn to those with Arcane abilities, and are always waiting for some misstep or lapse of concentration to provide them with some 'entertainment'

Pity the poor soul then, who loses control of their Arcane energies in such places...

The following Miscast table is recommended optional, and is designed to replace the existing Miscast rules found in the *Dracula's America: Shadows of the West* rulebook. All players should agree to the table's use before the game begins as it can be a mite unforgiving (but often amusing – or at least for those not suffering its effects)!

Whenever a model tries to Cast an Arcane Power (whether within or outside the Hunting Grounds) and they generate a Miscast, roll a D10 on the following table instead of applying the usual rules for Miscasts.

MISCAST TABLE		
D10 Roll	**Miscast**	**Notes**
1	Spirit-Eater!	The Caster's spirit is sucked from their body and devoured by a lurking entity – this means instant death in a Campaign!
2–5	Free at Last!	An Abyssal Entity uses the dissipating energy to breach the walls of the Hunting Grounds – roll a D3 to determine what: 1 = Lesser Abyssal. 2 = Minor Abyssal. 3 = Major Abyssal. The Abyssal is an NPC, and is placed D6+1" away from the Caster in a random direction. It uses the appropriate rules given on page 16. If you are attempting to Cast the Summon Power alongside the optional rules for rogue Abyssals given earlier and roll this result, then follow those rules and treat this result as a roll of Possession instead.
6–9	Arcane Detonation!	The Caster suffers the usual effects of a Miscast (i.e. they become Shaken or Downed). In addition, all other models within 3" of them are struck by a blast of wild Arcane power and must make a 5+ Save.
10	Possession!	An Abyssal Entity takes control of the Caster's body for a brief instant – the model immediately performs either a Shoot (using the best Weapon they have if there is a choice), or Fight Action (if it has no eligible ranged Weapons) exactly as if it were an NPC, and then receives a Done Token. Remember that is must make this Action even if it technically has no Actions left this Activation! If there are no viable Targets, the model will Move in a random direction instead.

SPIRIT CREATURES – A BESTIARY

Roll 1D10 on this table to determine what kind of Spirit Creature has followed you through into the physical realm.

All Spirit Creatures are Supernatural Entities, and follow the usual NPC rules.

SPIRIT CREATURES TABLE	
D10 Roll	**Spirit Creature**
1	Manitou
2	Nature Spirit
3	Mothman
4	Ghost-Witch
5	Flying Head
6	Angry Spirit
7	Wendigo
8	Bukwus
9	Thunder-Bird
10	Spirit-Eater

Manitou

Though occasionally seen prowling the physical world, Manitous are in fact residents of the Hunting Grounds – where they are the undisputed apex-predator!

	Base Size	Move	Grit	Special
MANITOU	40mm	6"	D10	Fearsome. Mean. Tough.

Nature Spirit

Nature Spirits take many forms, but usually assume a large, vaguely humanoid shape composed of the natural element to which it is attuned.

	Base Size	Move	Grit	Special
NATURE SPIRIT	40mm	4"	D8	Fearsome.

Roll a further D4 on the table below to determine what kind of Nature Spirit you have encountered. Regardless of the variety, all Nature Spirits have the following basic profile:

NATURE SPIRIT TYPE GENERATOR	
D4 Roll	**Spirit**
1	Air Spirit: An Air Spirit has Flying.
2	Water Spirit: A Water Spirit ignores water-based terrain and is 'Ornery.
3	Earth Spirit: An Earth Spirit is always treated as wearing Boilerplate, but does not reduce its Move rate.
4	Fire Spirit: All non-Entity models within 2" of a Fire Spirit at the end of its Activation must make a 5+ Save.

OPPOSITE Spirit Creature: Ghost-Witch

Mothman

So-called because their shadowy form most often takes the shape of a vaguely insect-like humanoid with large red eyes, a Mothman is a kind of 'death-omen' whose appearance always foreshadows doom to those in the vicinity.

	Base Size	Move	Grit	Special
MOTHMAN	25mm	6"	D8	Flying. Fearsome. A Mothman will always make random Moves, and will never engage or attack another model – nor can it be attacked, engaged or harmed in any way, besides the Arcane Power Banish. All models within 6" of this model suffer an additional -1 Save Modifier.

Ghost-Witch

Shrieking female phantoms, Ghost-Witches are the subject of many legends from many different Native American tribes – yet all agree that misfortune and sorrow follow in their wake...

	Base Size	Move	Grit	Special
GHOST-WITCH	25mm	4"	D8	Ethereal. Fearsome. Tough. A Ghost-Witch will always Shoot the closest visible model within 12" instead of moving if applicable. This Attack is never modified and can never Jam. If the Target fails their Save they suffer no harm but gain a Curse token instead (see the Curse Arcane Power).

Flying Head

Also known simply as 'Whirlwinds' in certain myths, Flying Heads are exactly that – unnaturally large, severed heads with a hunger for fresh meat and the ability to summon a vortex of supernatural wind.

FLYING HEAD	Base Size	Move	Grit	Special
25mm	8"	D6	Flying. Fearsome. All models within 3" of the Flying Head suffer a -1 Die Modifier to their Shooting Tests.

Angry Spirit

Many Spirits have been driven insane over the millennia, and have forgotten their previous life as mortals. Some were never alive, and simply have an irrational hatred of the living!

ANGRY SPIRIT	Base Size	Move	Grit	Special
25mm	4"	D6	Ethereal. Fearsome. Tough.

Wendigo

Feral Spirits of winter and hunger, the Wendigo are the twisted souls of desperate men and women who committed cannibalism in life. Now, they possess a craving for fresh meat that can never be sated – a Wendigo with the scent of fresh blood in its nostrils enters a frenzied state!

WENDIGO	Base Size	Move	Grit	Special
25mm	6"	D8	Fearsome. 'Ornery. Mean whilst Fighting a Shaken opponent.

Bukwus

One of the strangest undead Spirits one might encounter in the Hunting Grounds, the Bukwus is the spirit of someone who drowned. They appear as a skeletal figure draped in river-weeds and constantly dripping water. Most horrifying of all is their ability to transform any living victim into a new Bukwus!

	Base Size	Move	Grit	Special
BUKWUS	25mm	4"	D8	Ethereal. Fearsome. Hard to Kill. Any non-Supernatural model Downed by a Bukwus in a Fight must score a Success on 1 Grit Die or immediately die! Replace the unfortunate model with a new Bukwus (if you have a model available) and remove it from its owner's Roster, following all rules for dead models.

Thunder-Bird

Huge, majestic spirits of the air; the Thunder-Birds create rumbling thunder with a beat of their mighty wings, and cause lightning to strike the ground with their shrieking cries – though this is a juvenile of the species, it is nevertheless an awe-inspiring sight!

	Base Size	Move	Grit	Special
THUNDER-BIRD	40mm	2D6" rolled each time it Moves	*	Flying. This model always moves in a random direction, ignoring all models and terrain at all times – it cannot be Attacked or harmed in any way, but may be affected by the Banish Arcane Power! If a double 1 is rolled for its random movement, it leaves play immediately. All models within 3" of a Thunder-Bird at the end of its random Move must make a 5+ Save from the random lightning bolts it generates.

Spirit-Eater

Thought by those with knowledge of such things to be entities from beyond even the known planes of existence, a Spirit-Eater appears as an amorphous mass of shadowy tendrils that twist and coil about a central 'maw'. It is driven by an unceasing hunger for Animus – whether plucked raw from the Hunting Grounds, or by consuming lesser Spirit creatures – however, the greatest delicacy for a Spirit-Eater is without doubt the soul of a living creature...

	Base Size	Move	Grit	Special
SPIRIT EATER	40mm	4"	D10	Ethereal. Fearsome. Automatically Succeeds all Saves it is called upon to make – instead, it will be pushed 1" directly away from its attacker in a straight line for every Success their Attacker scored. Can only be removed from play via the Banish Arcane Power. If the Spirit-Eater ever wins a Fight by 2 or more, the loser must Succeed a 1 Die Nerve Test or die automatically (that's right – the model is dead and gone!) if they Fail their Save.

New Weapons

Musket (Basic Weapon, $1)

Though obsolete even before the end of the Civil War thanks to their slow reloading time, there are still some stubborn (or desperate) souls using these antique weapons.

This new Weapon can be taken by any Posse from any Faction.

Weapon	Ranges			Jam	Notes
	S	M	L		
MUSKET	6"	12"	18"	Auto	Rifle. Automatically Jams after each shot. Your Posse may have as many Muskets as you wish, regardless of any other restrictions on the number of certain Weapons you can field — though they still take up 1 Weapon 'slot' for the user. In addition, Dark Confederacy Revenants may be armed with a Musket instead of a Pistol.

Throwing Weapon (Special Weapon, $1)

A well-aimed knife, tomahawk or throwing star has spelt the end for many an unsuspecting gunslinger!

A model may have up to 3 Throwing Weapons in total, which all count as a single Weapon slot. Each Throwing Weapon is one use per game, so mark them off on your Roster Sheet as they are used — it is assumed that the owner retrieves all its used Throwing Weapons at the end of this game, ready for the next.

A model can throw one of these weapons up to 6" at the end of any Move, counting as part of that Action. It cannot be used if you moved into Contact with an enemy, however! The thrower makes an unmodified 1 Die Shooting Test to determine if it hits, and the Target Saves as usual.

CLOSE COMBAT WEAPONS

A model may only carry one Close Combat Weapon. These count as Weapons in all respects, you may equip any eligible model with a Close Combat Weapon instead of or as well as any Ranged Weapons if you wish!

Spear ($3, Native American and Chinese Posses only)

A primitive but effective weapon consisting of a sharp blade on the end of a sturdy shaft, in this age of guns only those who still hold on to the old ways would use a spear!

In a Fight, the user may re-roll any one of their Dice if they are the Defender.

Sword ($5)

In a time when even the most skilled warrior can die to a bullet from a coward's gun, there are still some who believe meeting your enemy blade-to-blade is the true measure of a fighter's worth. Whether wielding a cavalry sabre or a Chinese longsword, these duellists harken back to a more 'civilised' age...

In a Fight, the user may re-roll any one of their Dice, whether Attacker or Defender.

Two-Handed Weapon ($7)

Certain brutal individuals prefer to put their trust in a weighty hammer used to bludgeon railway spikes into place, a lumberjack's axe, or some other kind of unwieldy – yet devastating – weapon.

This Item imposes a -1 Die Modifier on all of its wielder's Fight Tests and they cannot also use a Derringer. However, an opponent Struck by it suffers a -1 Save Modifier.

New Arcane Powers

SPIRITUALISM ARCANE POWERS

These Powers are available to all Arcanists, and can be learned by Advancing or even taken as one of an Arcanist's initial Powers if you wish.

Spirit-Jump

Difficulty 2.

Like a stone skipping across the surface of a creek, in the blink of an eye you disappear into the Hunting Grounds before reappearing in the physical world some distance away from where you started!

The Caster is immediately placed anywhere within 6" and LOS of its current position, but no closer than 3" to an enemy model. Remember that it effectively remains in its current realm – so if it Casts this Power while in the Hunting Grounds then it ends this Action still in the Hunting Grounds.

Spirit-Grasp

Difficulty 3.

You sense the presence of nearby creatures in the spirit realm, and with a forceful grasping motion you wrench them into the physical plane before you.

When this Power is Cast from the physical realm, all models (friend or foe), and/or Loot counters within 2" of the Caster (but not terrain elements) lose any Spirit Tokens they may have and are now considered to be in the physical realm in all respects. This Power cannot be Cast from within the Hunting Grounds!

Planar Portal

Difficulty 3.

You weaken the barriers between our world and the Hunting Grounds for a split second, allowing you and those allies nearby to step effortlessly between the planes.

Place a 50mm diameter 'portal' centred over the Caster. All friendly models even partially under the marker are transported to or from the Hunting Grounds (as appropriate) along with the Caster.

SHAMANISM ARCANE POWERS

These Powers are only available to non-Hired Gun Arcanists of the Skinwalker Tribes Faction.

Shadow Dance

Difficulty 1.

As you finish the sacred chant, the outline of your fellow warrior begins to fade and ripple like a desert heat-haze, becoming indistinct and hard to single out from their surroundings...

Choose a friendly model within LOS and 6" of the Caster (including themselves!). If this Power is Cast successfully, all enemies that Shoot at the affected model suffer an additional -1 Die Modifier until the end of the current Game Turn. However, the affected model will never count as the closest enemy model.

Communion

Difficulty 2.

Reaching out with your spirit, you enter the mind of the creature before you and take control – its body is now merely an extension of your will!

If this Power is Cast successfully, choose one NPC model within LOS and 12" of the Caster. The chosen model and the Caster then each roll one Grit Die. If the Caster scores equal to or higher than the Target, you may immediately perform 1 legal Action with that model (using any of its special attacks and/or abilities) as if it were part of your Posse. You cannot make the affected model go on Lookout. If the Caster scores lower than the Target, then there is no effect and the Power fails.

Entangle

Difficulty 3.
Imploring the Spirits of Nature to heed your call, you cause thick vines and roots to burst from the ground and ensnare your enemies in their thorny grasp.

Choose an enemy model within LOS and 12" of the Caster that is at ground level (that is, stood on the table-top itself) and not in or on top of a building. If this Power is Cast successfully, the affected model always counts as being in rough ground whenever it Moves until the end of the current Game Turn.

DIABOLISM ARCANE POWERS

These Powers are only available to non-Hired Gun Arcanists of the Crossroads Cult Faction.

The Pact

Difficulty 3.
Choose a friendly Summoned model within 6" of the Caster and that is not Down. If this Power is Cast successfully, the Targeted model becomes Shaken (or Downed if already Shaken), and the Caster removes their Shaken token if they have one. Alternatively, you may reverse the effects and have the Caster take the Damage and the Targeted model remove their Shaken marker instead if you wish!

Infernal Gateway

Difficulty 3.
Choose a friendly Summoned model within 12" of the Caster. If this Power is Cast successfully, remove the Targeted model from play and then immediately place it anywhere within LOS and 3" of the Caster that is no closer than 1" to an enemy model.

Diabolic Command

Difficulty 2.
Choose a friendly Summoned model within LOS and 9" of the Caster. If this Power is Cast Successfully, the Targeted model may immediately perform 1 legal Action of your choice and even if it is already marked as Done – immediately after resolving this Action, the model becomes Shaken – or is Downed if already Shaken! This Power cannot be Cast on a Downed model.

New Factions

THE FORSAKEN

"I just want you boys to know – I didn't ask for any of this! I used to be a regular feller like you before this nightmare began...

Whoah boys, now there's no need to do this – lower them guns! Look, see my uniform – I was a Lieutenant in the 7th! I'm one of you, I swear. We didn't mean to kill them folks back in Deadwood, it was an accident! Jus' lemme explain...

...Ah c'mon now, yer makin' me angry... And y'wouldn't like me when I'm angry..."

Lieutenant Sam Butler, formerly of the 7th Cavalry
(Seconds before the Black Bull Massacre, 1877)

Joining this Faction makes your Posse a rare breed – non-Native Americans with the ability to transform into monstrous beasts! However, unlike true Skinwalkers, this is involuntary and the result of some dark curse or abominable Arcane accident, and you must constantly struggle to control the beast within...

Native American Posses may not join this Faction!

Faction Benefit: Accursed

In addition, at the start of each game but before Deployment, randomly determine two non-Hired Gun models in your Posse. These models are Accursed for the duration of this game (after which they return to normal), replace these models with suitably monstrous Beast Forms on a 40mm base.

An Accursed model is Supernatural and has Lead-Belly and Fearsome in this form.

An Accursed cannot use any Weapons or Gear, Cast Arcane Powers or ride a Horse – any unusable items the model had when it became Accursed are not lost however, and are returned to the model automatically after the game is over (should they survive!).

In addition, being a berserk beast, it does not count for Controlling objectives and cannot carry Loot or hold Bystanders.

OPPOSITE The Forsaken: Cavalryman

An Accursed Moves 6", and in a Fight it gains a +2 Die Modifier (whether Attacker or Defender).

At the start of an Accursed's Activation in which it is Shaken, and before it can do anything else, it must roll a D6:

- On a roll of 2+, it may be Activated as normal by the owning player.
- On a roll of 1, it becomes frenzied! The model counts as an NPC for the duration of this Activation only, and follows all the appropriate behavioural rules as if it were the NPC Phase – it may even attack 'friendly' models in its maddened state!

If Downed, an Accursed remains in its monstrous form and follows all the usual rules for Downed models. It does not roll to see if it becomes frenzied while it is Down.

Faction Benefit: Fugitives

As former members of the 7th Cavalry, Forsaken Posses may buy Horses – not including Appaloosas – at half cost (rounding up), and may even buy them for a starting Posse.

However, they are constantly hunted by the other Factions for various reasons, so Forsaken Posses are always Outlawed in a Campaign (see page 64), and can never pay Blood Money to remove this status.

THE SHADOW DRAGON TONG

"Stay away from them there Chinese, boy – y'hear me?

Oh sure, they act real polite-like, an' look like they wouldn't say boo to a goose – but lemme tell ya, they's more 'ornery 'n a rattler an' twice as poisonous!

Hey, don' lookit me like that, boy – I'm tellin' ya, I seen them fellas walk through walls like they wasn't there, appearin' outta the shadows from nowhere; an' I seen jus' one o' them take on five men bare-handed n' leave those tough ol' cowpokes sittin' in the dust spittin' teeth an' blood!

An' worse'n that – they took my job on the Deadwood Line – worked twice as hard as you or I, or anyone I met ever could, an' all fer half the pay... An' now they's got their fingers in ev'ry pie in town – all in the space o' jus' a few months!

I tell ya, boy, them folk ain't nat'ral, not like decent, upstandin' Americans such as you n' me!

...Hey, pass me that bottle aggin..."

Unknown drunk, overheard in Nuttal's Number 10 Saloon
(Deadwood City, 1878)

Joining this Faction makes your Posse the mysterious agents of the Shadow Dragon Tong – a secretive organisation with fingers in many pies, and whose will is enforced by lethal martial artists with a sinister connection to the spirit realms...

Only Chinese Posses may join this Faction.

Faction Benefit: Guilao

Two models in your Posse must become Guilao ('Ghost-Men') when you join this Faction.

Guilao Move 6", are Supernatural, Ethereal, and roll an extra Die in a Fight for each '1' rolled by their opponent.

However, they may never be given any Weapons except Bows (even though they are not Native Americans), Throwing Weapons, and Close Combat Weapons. They may not be given Derringers, the Guilao stick to the ancient martial traditions of their ancestors.

If a Guilao dies, you must have another non-Hired Gun model in your Posse become a new Guilao, as long as you never have more than two Guilao in your Posse at any one time. Any now-unusable items are lost.

Faction Benefit: Tong Tattoos

When a Veteran or Hero member of this Posse Advances, instead of rolling on the Advancement table they may purchase an Animus-ink Tattoo. This adds +1 to their personal Infamy. You must also pay the appropriate Dollar cost from your Stash, and each model may have only one Tattoo. Note any Tattoos along with the bearer's Skills on your Roster Sheet.

- **Dragon ($4):** The bearer may breathe mystical flames as a Shoot Action, once per game. This is a Fire Corridor attack with a Range of 4".
- **Monkey ($2):** The bearer rolls 2 Dice and takes the best result when making a Save caused by Falling.
- **Snake ($6):** If an enemy model Disengages successfully from this model, they must make a 5+ Save as if the Disengage Test was Failed. If the Test was actually Failed, they must make a 6+ Save instead!
- **Tiger ($4):** The bearer adds +2" to their Move rate when on foot and if performing a Charge.

OPPOSITE The Shadow Dragon Tong: Enforcer

SKINWALKER TRIBE THEMES

The Skinwalker Tribes are a loose confederation of various Native American Peoples, united under the leadership of the mysterious Shaman known only as White Raven – from the Sioux, Pawnee, and Cheyenne of the plains and prairies, to the Blackfoot, Seminoles, and Crow of the woodlands and mountains, and the Apache and Navajo of the deserts – amongst many others.

These are optional rules that allow players with a Skinwalker Tribes Posse to further theme their model collections around these and many other Native American Peoples if their opponents agree. I really do recommend doing some research on the various Native American cultures, as this is a complex and fascinating subject that we regrettably can only cover in an incredibly limited fashion here – as always, feel free to amend or mix these rules or even come up with your own!..

You must decide on one (and only one!) Theme before building your Posse, and this cannot be changed between games if you are taking part in a Campaign.

The Plains and Prairie Tribes

Proud Horsemen

Plains and Prairie Tribes Posses may buy Horses – not including Appaloosas and so on – at half cost (rounding up), and may even buy them for a starting Posse.

Buffalo Form

Instead of choosing a Wolf or Bear Form, a Plains or Prairie Tribes Skinwalker may choose the Buffalo Form instead. They follow all the basic rules for Skinwalkers, and gain the Bull-Rush and Tough Skills when in Beast Form.

OPPOSITE Spirit Creature: Flying Head

The Woodland and Mountain Tribes

Self-Sufficient

Woodland and Mountain Tribe Novice and Veteran models treat their Grit as one Rank better when making Nerve Tests (including Bottle Checks). So, a Novice counts as a Veteran if called upon to make a Nerve Test.

Friends to the Sasquatch

Woodland and Mountain Tribe Posses may take a Sasquatch as a Hired Gun! This model follows all the usual Hired Gun rules, and is under the player's direct control. It has the following rules, which are slightly different to those for an NPC Sasquatch:

SASQUATCH	To Hire	Retainer	Rank/Grit
	$22	$4	Veteran
Special	40mm Base. Supernatural. Lead-Belly. Fearsome. Gains Mean and 'Ornery while Shaken. Ignores penalty for moving through forested rough terrain. Does not need Weapons or Gear, and cannot be given any! Rolls for Injuries and Advances normally.		

The Desert Tribes

Elusive Warriors

Non-Hired Gun Desert Tribe models (including Bear-Form Skinwalkers) Move 5" on foot instead of 4".

Spiritual Guidance)

A Desert Tribes Posse may only have one Skinwalker model instead of the usual two.

However, one other non-Hired Gun model must become a Shaman instead and at no charge. This model becomes an Arcanist, and one of their three chosen Powers must be Banish.

Should your Shaman ever die, then you must choose another eligible model to be your new Shaman. They gain the benefits listed above in addition to their existing Weapons, Skills etc.

NEW CAMPAIGN RULES

NEW SKILL LISTS

The following new Skill Lists are available to all Posses from all Factions.

Riding Skills

\	\	RIDING SKILLS TABLE
D6 Roll	**Skill**	**Notes**
1	Expert Rider	While mounted, this model may ignore rough terrain as it Moves.
2	Long-Rider	While mounted, this model may add +D4" to its Move rate, rolled before moving the model. On a natural roll of '1' on the Die, the model is thrown by their mount instead — place it 1" away from the horse and make a 5+ Save on its behalf.
3	Leaping Dismount	When it dismounts, place this model in any viable position within 3" of its horse instead of in Contact with it. In addition, this model may Dismount at the end of a Move Action rather than at the start if you wish. You may even use this Skill to engage an enemy model, following all usual rules (Charging etc)!
4	Piercing Whistle	As an Action, this model may whistle for its horse if it is currently on foot. Immediately place their horse in Contact with this model, regardless of where it was on the table at the start of this Action. Common sense should be applied regarding exactly where the horse can go, if it cannot reach its rider, it must be placed as close as possible to their position. So you can't have your horse magically appear on the third storey of a building, for example! You can also use this Skill to bring back your horse if it fled the table earlier in the game (though not if it fell as a Casualty).
5	Trick-Rider	If Shot at, this model (including its Horse!) benefits from Cover while it is mounted.
6	Cavalryman	This model ignores all enemy models that are on foot when it Moves while mounted, but cannot end a Move within 1" of an enemy unless it is deliberately engaging them. In addition, while mounted this model gains an extra +1 Die Modifier when Charging a Defender on foot (for a bonus of +2!).

Leadership Skills

These Skills are unusual, in that only your Posse's Boss may use them. If a model somehow stops being your Boss for any reason but is still part of your Posse, then they may no longer use these Skills!

D6 Roll	Skill	Notes
	LEADERSHIP SKILLS TABLE	
1	Strategist	At the start of each game involving this model, after normal Deployment is completed you may immediately re-deploy up to half of your models that are currently on the table, following the usual Deployment rules for the Scenario.
		Where multiple opposing Posses have a model with this Skill, the players must Roll-Off with the winner deciding the order in which these re-deployments are carried out.
2	Ruthless (If you prefer, you can think of this as 'Beloved'!)	Once per Game Turn, when this model is Attacked (via Shooting or in a Fight) and must make a Save, you may have any one unengaged, non-Down friendly model within 2" and LOS take the Save (and any consequences!) instead.
3	Smarts	While this model leads your Posse, you may add +1 to the result of any and all Roll-Offs you make against the opposing player(s). This applies both before and during a game!
4	Disciplinarian	This model may choose to automatically pass or Fail the first Bottle Check it makes on behalf of its Posse in each Game.
5	Motivator	Once per Activation, this model may spend an Action to 'motivate' a visible friendly model within 6". The motivated model immediately performs a free Move Action, following all usual rules for Charging – it does not receive a Done marker after making this Action, and you may even use this Skill on a model that is already marked as Done. The motivated model may not use the Slick Skill, and a Shaken Accursed of the Forsaken Faction does not have to Test to see if it becomes frenzied!
6	Tactician	During each Draw Phase, you may draw an extra card than normal from your Deck if you wish, as long as this model is on the table and not Down.

OPPOSITE The Forsaken: Sharpshooter

NEW GEAR

Unless otherwise noted, any Faction may Search for and/or buy the following new Gear in a Campaign.

ITEM PRICE LIST			
Basic Weapons		**Close Combat Weapons**	
Musket	$1	Spear	$3, Native American & Chinese Posses only
Special Weapons		Sword	$5
Throwing Weapons	$1	Two-Handed Weapon	$7
Supernatural Gear		Coup-Stick*	$8, Native American Posses only
Brimstone Chalk*	$6	**Horses and Gear**	
Coup-Stick*	$8, Native American Posses only	Warhorse*	$15
Dreamcatcher*	$25	*Uncommon Item	
Tome of Binding*	$18	Supernatural Gear is only used in a Dracula's America Campaign, but is included here for completeness.	
Vial of Animus	Cannot be purchased, only created		

Brimstone Chalk

Rumoured to be created from ashes gathered from the first circle of the Abyss, this stick of black chalk is shot through with yellowish veins and is said to possess a link to that hellish realm and the creatures that dwell there...

As an Action, the user draws a Summoning Circle on the ground – represent this with a 40mm diameter marker centred under them. The Circle remains in play until a new Circle is drawn by a model from the same Posse, whereupon the current one disappears. When a model in your Posse Casts the Summon Arcane Power, the Entity may be placed fully within the Circle regardless of its position relative to the Summoner – i.e., even if it is more than 3" away from them and out of their LOS.

This Item may not be used within the Hunting Grounds (who knows what you might call forth?).

Coup-Stick

To most, this wooden staff festooned with feathers and other trinkets is little more than a curiosity. To the Skinwalker Tribes, these seemingly simple objects are imbued with powerful Medicine that is the bane of creatures from the Hunting Grounds.

A Coup-Stick is a Close Combat Weapon that can only be used in a Dracula's America Campaign. If the user wins a Fight against an Entity and strikes them, that Entity suffers a -1 Save Modifier.

Dreamcatcher

This mystical artefact is said to capture the soul of a mortal at the very moment of death and return it safely to its body – completely healed!

A model may only have a single Dreamcatcher at a time. If the bearer should die, the magic within the Dreamcatcher returns their spirit to their body and the model suffers no ill effects whatsoever. If a model dies due to suffering a duplicate Lasting Injury, they also ignore the second Injury (i.e. the one that would have killed them).

A Dreamcatcher only has enough magic for one use, after which it is useless and removed from your Roster.

Tome of Binding

Copied from the original volume – reputedly written many years ago by Edward Crowley himself – this book, bound in the leathery hide of an Abyssal Behemoth, can only be found in the possession of the most deranged of cultists. Within its yellowing pages are found detailed descriptions of the myriad Abyssal beings the Grand Magister has encountered over the years – their true names, habits, and weaknesses. The reader is better able to bind such entities to their will.

This Item may only be used by a Magister of the Crossroads Cult Faction.

It allows the bearer to have up to two Summoned Creatures in play at once instead of one, but following all other rules for Summoning as detailed in the *Dracula's America: Shadows of the West* rulebook.

Vial of Animus

Gathered at great risk from within the Hunting Grounds, Animus is highly-prized by Arcanists and dabblers in spiritualism alike – however, such power often comes at an unexpected price...

A Vial of Animus is an item of Supernatural Gear which can only be given to an Arcanist. It cannot be purchased, only created, and may not be sold on.

An Arcanist may use this Item when it declares a Cast Action. The user discards the Vial and treats its Grit as 1 Rank better for the duration of that Casting Test. A Hero-Ranked model gains a +1 Die Modifier instead. However, if a Miscast is generated you must roll two Dice on the Miscast table and take the lowest result!

This item may be used in combination with a Grimoire, however you can only use one Vial per Casting Test.

Warhorse

Whether the well-trained animals used by the US Cavalry, or the spirited Stallions ridden to war by Native American Braves; a Warhorse is tough and well-used to the chaos of battle.

Counts as a Horse in all respects, but has Grit D8.

NEW HIRED GUNS

Unless noted otherwise, any Faction may hire the following new models in a Campaign.

Bounty Hunter

Pragmatic and ruthless individuals, Bounty Hunters come from all walks of life and all have their own stories to tell. This Hired Gun can represent a grizzled Texas Ranger or scar-faced ex-Confederate Officer, amongst other diverse types!

BOUNTY HUNTER	To Hire	Retainer	Rank/Grit
	$18	$5	Veteran
Special	This model has random Skills, Injuries and equipment that are generated immediately after you have hired them: First, randomly generate 1 Gumption Skill, and either 1 Shooting Skill or 1 Fighting Skill. Then roll a D6 to determine the Weapon loadout they start with: 1: Pistol, 2: Rifle, 3: Shotgun, 4: Two Pistols, 5: Rifle and Pistol, 6: Shotgun and Pistol Finally, roll a D4 to determine the Lasting Injury they start with: 1: Old Wound, 2: One-Eyed, 3: Limp, 4: Weakened		

Exorcist

Exorcists may be specialist members of the Clergy or Medicine Men with an instinctive power over the denizens of the Hunting Grounds.

EXORCIST	To Hire	Retainer	Rank/Grit
	$11	$3	Novice
Special	This model knows the Banish and Spirit-Grasp Arcane Powers (but is not an Arcanist). Armed with a Pistol.		

Frontiersman

Men and Women who find it hard to fit-in amongst the crowded towns often choose the hard, solitary life of an explorer out on the Frontier. They are constantly pushing the boundaries of civilisation in search of new, unspoilt territories...

FRONTIERSMAN	To Hire	Retainer	Rank/Grit
	$16	$4	Veteran
Special	At the end of each Purchase Phase (i.e. before calculating your new Infamy), you may roll 1D6 on behalf of this model if you wish. On a 1 they vanish into the wilderness and are never seen again. On a 6 you may randomly generate a new Territory (see page 54) and add it to your Roster if you wish and are able to do so. Armed with a Rifle.		

Gatling Gun

The Gatling Gun is a military weapon that first saw use during the closing years of the Civil War. However, it can now be found all across Dracula's America – whether blunting the attack of a pack of vampiric townsfolk, or taking down a rampaging werebeast!

A Gatling Gun and its Crew are a single model sharing one 50mm base, following all the normal rules for Hired Guns. In addition, the model cannot be given any other Weapons or Gear, nor ride a Horse!

GATLING GUN TEAM	To Hire	Retainer	Rank/Grit
	$20	$5	Novice
Special	50mm Base, Team Weapon, Wall of Lead (see text box, page 45). Armed with a Gatling Gun.		

GATLING GUN SPECIAL RULES: TEAM WEAPON

The Gatling Gun and its Crew count as one model for the purposes of Deployment, Posse size (including calculating Bottle Checks and number of cards in your Hand), Reactions, and Activations. In a Campaign, it also counts as a single model when generating its Injuries and/or Advances.

A Gatling Gun Team can perform any of the usual Actions, with a Move rate of 3" and LOS being determined using the barrels of the Gun itself and by the direction they are pointing. However, a Gatling Gun can never Move to engage/Charge an enemy model, nor try to Disengage under any circumstances. It cannot be Shoved.

It may never climb or leap, nor drag Bystanders along. You will also need to exercise some common sense regarding where the Gun will fit – so no manhandling it through windows or over stacks of barrels, for example. It's a heavy-duty piece of kit, after all!

When Targeted by Shooting, the Gun always counts as having Cover (as the Crew instinctively shield themselves from enemy fire using the body of the Gun itself).

A Gatling Gun does not suffer Damage in the usual way – instead, it has 4 Hit Points. Each time it suffers a 'Shaken' result, it loses 1 Hit Point. Each time it suffers a 'Downed' result, it loses 2 Hit Points. Each time it suffers a 'Removed as a Casualty' result, it loses 3 Hit Points. Upon losing all its Hit Points, it then falls as a Casualty.

GATLING GUN SPECIAL RULES: WALL OF LEAD

After declaring they will fire the Gatling Gun but before resolving the attack, the player must first roll 1D6:

D6 Roll	Effect	Notes
WALL OF LEAD TABLE		
1	Ke-rack!	The Gatling Gun suffers a catastrophic misfire, and does not Shoot – it gains two Jammed tokens and cannot be fired again until both are cleared.
2	Clunk!	Something goes wrong, and the Gatling Gun does not Shoot – it gains a Jammed token and cannot be fired again until the Jam is cleared.
3+	Ready to go!	The Gun fires as normal – see below.

When it fires, the Gatling Gun projects a Wall of Lead to its front – imagine a straight line extending a full 12" from the left side of the Gun's base, then do the same for the right side. It may help to look down on the Gun from above to determine this. Solid obstructions of greater than 2" high/wide block the Wall of Lead.

The Wall of Lead is the area in between these two lines.

All visible models, friend or foe, whose centre of base lies completely within the Wall of Lead are Hit automatically and must make a 6+ Save.

Any visible model within the Wall of Lead but whose centre of base is not fully within it, or who have cover of 2" or less high/wide intervening between them and the Gun, are only potential Targets.

The Gatling Gun Team rolls its Grit Die for each such model – a Success indicates that the potential Target has been Hit, as above.

Medium

A Medium is one of those rare individuals actually able to perceive and communicate with spirits. Though this is by no means an exact science, their ability to call upon such supernatural help can give their allies an advantage, and they are much in demand.

MEDIUM	To Hire	Retainer	Rank/Grit
	$10	$3	Novice
Special	This model rolls on the Vision Quest table (see page 50) – treating a roll of 1 as an 'Unworthy' result – before Deployment in each game to determine what kind of Spirit has answered their call. At the end of the game, the Totem Spirit vanishes. Armed with a Pistol.		

OPPOSITE Hired Gun: Gatling Gun

Pinkerton Agent

The motto of the Pinkerton Detective Agency is "We never sleep" – as thralls of Dracula, this was never more true! The Pinkertons are masters of espionage (particularly the art of disguise) and counter-espionage, and if the rumours are correct, are not adverse to a little 'moonlighting' for other employers besides the President...

PINKERTON AGENT	To Hire	Retainer	Rank/Grit
	$16	$4	Veteran
Special	Supernatural. Move 6". This model is not Deployed normally – instead, it is left off-table. Starting from Turn 3, at the start of any of your Solo Activations you may declare the Pinkerton is revealing themselves – place it anywhere on the table that is no closer than 6" to an enemy model – this counts as the Pinkerton's Activation, but cannot trigger Reactions. If it does not reveal itself before the end of the game, then it does not count as taking part in that game! Until it reveals itself, the model does not count as in-play. Armed with a Pistol.		

Spirit-Walker

A Spirit-Walker may be a talented Spiritualist or Native American Shaman – whatever their background, they possess the ability to move between the material and spirit realms at will!

SPIRIT-WALKER	To Hire	Retainer	Rank/Grit
	$10	$2	Novice
Special	This model is, as the name implies, a Spirit-Walker. It may freely pass between the Hunting Grounds and the physical realm as described earlier in these rules. Armed with a Pistol.		

VISION QUESTS & SPIRIT TOTEMS

Any one non-Hired Gun model in your Posse of Veteran Rank or higher may choose to go on a Vision Quest between games in this Campaign. Just so we're clear, only one eligible model per Posse may embark on a Vision Quest each Campaign Turn!

It must have survived the previous game and cannot Advance, take part in Encounters or Search for Uncommon Items for the rest of this Campaign Phase.

In the Advancement Phase, roll 1D8 on behalf of the model on the Vision Quest table below to determine which Spirit (if any) becomes the model's Totem – once a model has found its Totem, it may never embark on another Vision Quest!

Native American models may choose to add or subtract 1 from their roll if they wish.

You can write a model's Totem down on your Roster Sheet, or place a suitable model or token with them during play as a reminder – these representations usually have no real presence in-game and cannot be interacted with in any way, nor do they count as 'models' for game purposes... But who wouldn't want to have a spectral raven or coyote following their models around?

VISION QUEST TABLE		
D8 Roll	Vision Quest	Notes
1	Lost in the Hunting Grounds!	The model's Spirit is cast adrift in the Hunting Grounds, or is devoured by a ravenous Entity — either way, the model is dead and removed from your Roster!
2	Unworthy	The model does not find its Spirit Totem this time, but may try again in future.
3	Wolf Spirit	When it enters the Hunting Grounds, a Wolf Spirit appears in Contact with this model but not any enemies. It counts as part of your Posse, but does not add a card to your Hand or count towards Bottle Checks. It disappears if it would leave the Hunting Grounds. If its 'master' leaves the Hunting Grounds, it will disappear and return the next time this model enters the Hunting Grounds — even if it previously fell as a Casualty. The profile is given below.
4	Bear Spirit	When this model enters the Hunting Grounds a Bear Spirit appears, following all the rules given for the Wolf Spirit, above.
5	Coyote Spirit	This model becomes a Spirit-Walker. If it is already a Spirit-Walker, treat this as a roll of 2.
6	Raven Spirit	While it is in the physical realm, this model may see and Attack enemy models in the Hunting Grounds. Similarly, while in the Hunting Grounds it may see and Attack enemies in the physical realm. However, such models may also see and Attack this model! All other rules for models with Spirit Tokens apply.
7	Ancestor Spirit	This model is protected by the spirit of an Ancestor. Each time it successfully makes a Save against a Shooting or Fighting attack and rolls the maximum number possible (for example, a ten on a D10), its attacker must immediately make a 5+ Save.
8	Horse Spirit	This model gains a Spirit Horse with a Move rate of 6". This horse can never be truly 'killed' and is always available to its owner in each game, but follows all the other rules for Horses. In addition, the Horse (and its rider, while mounted) count as Ethereal.

WOLF SPIRIT	Base Size	Move	Grit	Special
	25mm	6"	D6	Supernatural. Entity.

BEAR SPIRIT	Base Size	Move	Grit	Special
	40mm	4"	D8	Supernatural. Entity. Fearsome.

INDIAN TERRITORY ENCOUNTERS

When playing in a Campaign set within the Indian Territory (as agreed upon by the players before starting the Campaign), you must generate Encounters from the lists that follow.

TWO OF A KIND ENCOUNTERS TABLE		
Two of a Kind	Encounter	Notes
1	Raid!	Screams carry towards you on the wind, and you race to investigate – you come upon a burning homestead, whose bloodied and terrified occupants are encircled by wildly whooping warriors! Skinwalker Tribe Posses may join the raid, earning +1 Infamy on a D6 score of 4+. Other Posses may leave the victims to their fate (in which case the Encounter ends now) or try to rescue them. If a rescue is attempted, 1 random model in your Posse must roll for Injury but you earn $10 from the grateful Settlers.
2	Sacred Ground	A tingling sensation of wild power fills you as you cross this area of wilderness. You must try to appease the Spirits inhabiting this holy place. Roll a D6, adding 1 to the result if you are a Skinwalker Tribe Posse, on a 4+ the Spirits are pleased – D3 models of your choice start the next game with a Bless token (see the Bless Arcane Power). On a score of 3 or less the Spirits are angered – D3 models of your choice must start the next game with a Curse token (see the Curse Arcane Power).
3	Open Range	A herd of cattle comes over the ridge, accompanied by two tired-looking Cowboys. They look like they could use a hand... If you wish, you may send up to two non-Supernatural models to join the Cowboys on the trail in an attempt to get these beeves to the nearest town. If you do, choose the 'volunteers' and roll a D3. The nominated models must miss a number of Campaign Turns (starting from the next one) equal to the number rolled, but for each Campaign Turn missed in this way each model earns you $D5 and grants them +1EXP, added to your Stash when they return to your Posse. While on this leave of absence they still count towards your Posse's maximum size!
4	Aftermath	You stumble across the smouldering ruins of a small homestead. The previous occupants are nowhere to be seen... Sifting through the ruins earns you $D6.
5	Lost in the Hunting Grounds!	Somehow, a member of your Posse gets separated from their comrades in the Hunting Grounds. Randomly select a surviving model in your Posse. This model must miss the rest of this Campaign Turn and the whole of the next. This model does however earn +D3 EXP for the experience!
6	Warring Tribes	Your Posse has inadvertently found themselves swept up in a great battle between rival tribes! Your Posse must either flee like cowards, or join the battle in favour of one side or the other. If you decide to fight your way out then there is no further effect. If you decide to aid one side or the other, roll a D6. If the score is Even, your side wins – D3 random models must roll for Injury, but you earn D3+1 EXP that can be distributed as you like amongst your models. If the score is Odd, your chosen side loses and D3 random models must make Injury rolls.

THREE OF A KIND ENCOUNTERS TABLE		
Three of a Kind	Encounter	Notes
1	Convergence!	You discover an area of major Convergence out in the wilderness — this will give your Posse a valuable edge over their enemies in the next battle! You find D3-1 Portions of Animus. In addition, D3 Models in your Posse (of your choice) may start the next game Deployed already within the Hunting Grounds if you wish.
2	Wandering Medicine Man	A gnarled old man hails you as you traverse a woodland path... Roll a D6 and add +2 if your Posse is of the Skinwalker Tribes Faction. On a score of 6 or above, the Medicine Man offers to help you — one model of your choice removes a single Lasting Injury it is currently suffering.
3	Collapsed Mine!	While travelling through a rocky area of Indian Territory, you hear muffled shouts for help. Following the sounds, you come across a ragged Prospector desperately clawing at a huge pile of fallen stone — he shouts that there was a cave-in and his fellow miners are now trapped somewhere under it all! You can send up to 4 models from your Posse to help out if you wish. Each such model should roll 1 Grit Die — on a Failure they fail to rescue anyone — if they rolled a 1 then they also cause a further collapse and must roll for Injury in addition. On a Success they rescue a trapped miner — if you rolled the maximum possible score then they rescue two miners! Earn $D3 for each miner you rescue. If you rescue 3 or more miners in total you also earn +1 Infamy.
4	Good Hunting	This area of Indian Territory is rich with abundant game of all kinds... You earn an extra $D8 from hunting the various animals found in the area. On a roll of 1 then a random model runs afoul of a Grizzly or some other predator, and must roll for Injury!
5	Abyssal Attack!	During a foray into the Hunting Grounds, your Posse is attacked as if from nowhere by ravening Abyssal Entities! After a ferocious battle, you manage to drive the creatures away. Roll a D3. This many randomly selected models from your Posse must roll for Injury immediately. However, each of these models gains 1 EXP (should they survive, of course!).
6	Lost Settlers	While exploring the Hunting Grounds, you come across a small group of bewildered folk wandering in the darkness — they seem to have no idea of where they are or how they got here! You may decide to abandon them to their fate, or escort them to safety in the physical realm. If you abandon them, there is no effect (though hopefully your Boss loses some sleep over this decision!). If you decide to rescue them, roll a D6: 1: the 'Settlers' turn out to be Trickster Spirits in disguise and D3 random models in your Posse have a Curse token (see the Curse Arcane Power in the main rulebook for details) at the start of your next game. 2–3: the 'Settlers' vanish with mocking laughter, but there is no other effect. 4–5: the Settlers are genuine, and incredibly grateful for the rescue! You earn $D10+2, and +1 Infamy. 6: the 'Settlers' turn out to be Trickster Spirits in disguise — taking a liking to your Posse, they lead them to an area of raw Ectoplasm before vanishing — add D3 Portions of Animus to your Stash.

FOUR OF A KIND ENCOUNTERS TABLE		
Four of a Kind	Encounter	Notes
1	Trainwreck	Following a thick plume of oily smoke, you come across a terrible scene of destruction — a locomotive lies ruined on its side by buckled rails, and tattered bodies are strewn about the wreckage. You may send up to 3 models to investigate the wreck — roll a D6 for each to see what they find: 1: Nothing of value. 2–3: Sundry small goods worth $D6. 4–5: Valuable cargo worth $D8. 6: A survivor — upon escorting them to safety you earn $D10 from their grateful family!
2	New Territory!	Your Posse has found an ancient trail leading to an unspoilt area not yet marked on any map! Immediately roll a D6 to generate a new Territory (see page 56), a roll of 1 indicates Badlands, a 2–5 indicates Farmland, and a 6 means you discover a new Claim.
3	Curious Spirit.	As your Posse ventures into the Hunting Grounds, a curious Spirit takes a sudden and inexplicable interest in one of your comrades... Randomly select a model in your Posse that does not already have a Spirit Totem. Roll on the Vision Quest table (see page 50) for that model, re-rolling results of 1 or 2 until you roll a 3 or better — they immediately gain the appropriate Spirit Totem!
4	Native American Settlement	Non-Skinwalker Posses must roll a D6 — if the result is an Odd number, or regardless of your roll if you are a Crossroads Cult Posse, then the locals take exception to your intrusion and chase you away. If the result is Even, the villagers are happy to trade. You may Sell-On up to three unwanted Weapons at full price rather than half (for example you can sell a Rifle for $5 rather than $2). If you are a Skinwalker Posse then you may also Purchase one of the following items/Weapons at half the normal Cost (rounded up): Appaloosa Horse, Bow, Coup-Stick, Dreamcatcher, Warhorse.
5	Railway Surveyor	As you cross an especially wild area of the Territory, you encounter an industrious looking man festooned with charts and maps. After a brief conversation, he offers to purchase some of your land on behalf of the Railroad! You may remove any non-Railroad Territory you control from your Roster and earn $D10x5. If you are a Skinwalker Tribe Posse you may kill the Surveyor instead and earn +1 Infamy.
6	Raw Ectoplasm	In an especially dark and forbidding area of the Hunting Grounds, your Posse stumbles upon a pulsing cloud of raw Ectoplasm — a very valuable find! You may send a single surviving model of your choice to harvest the Ectoplasm if you wish. Add D6 Portions of Animus to your Stash — if you roll a 1, the model falls victim to a Spirit-Eater lurking in ambush nearby and is dead — needless to say, no Animus is collected! If you roll a 6, the model collects enough Ectoplasm to allow your Posse to keep some for themselves. Add a Vial of Animus to your Stash, in addition to the 6 Portions!

Territory

Out on the Frontier, a man or woman must fight for every scrap of land they can get – whether against jealous rivals, Native tribes or just the harsh elements themselves, Territory is not just a place to live. It's a symbol of status and a measure of your determination to survive whatever the cost! In Dracula's America, it can also represent a new life; a new beginning away from the war and horror stalking the Nation...

Small wonder, then, that folks will gladly put their lives at stake to protect what is theirs!

Generating Territory

Each Posse randomly generates five Territories at the start of a Campaign by rolling a D10 five times on the table below. It is possible to generate multiple copies of the same Territory.

OPPOSITE The Shadow Dragon Tong: Guilao

THE TERRITORY CHART

D10 Roll	Territory	Worth	Notes
		TERRITORY CHART	
1	Badlands	0	It may be an inhospitable spit of land... But it's your land, dammit!
2	Farmland	1	Not an earthly paradise by any means, but a little hard work will bring reward...
3	Ranch	2	A nice parcel of land, with plenty of open range for the cattle and horses!
4	Stagecoach Route	D3	A nice money-maker – if it weren't for all the Outlaws! Roll for each Stagecoach Route you control at the end of the Campaign to calculate its Worth
5	Outpost	3	A little off the beaten track, but somebody's always passin' through.
6	Railroad	D4	Ah, the wonders of steam – ain't progress grand?! Roll for each Railroad you control at the end of the Campaign to calculate its Worth.
7	Settlement	4	Small, but perfectly formed...
8.	Claim	D5	One day soon you're gonna strike it rich... You just know it... Roll for each Claim you control at the end of the Campaign to calculate its Worth.
9	Town	5	Now we're talkin'! Always new folk around town, bringin' their money with 'em
10	Mine	D6	The motherlode is right beneath your feet – you can almost smell the wealth! Roll for each Mine you control at the end of the Campaign to calculate its Worth.

STAKING TERRITORY

Before each game, every player taking part must Stake one Territory on the outcome if able to do so.

The winner of the game keeps their Territory and also takes 1 other Territory of their choice that was Staked by an opponent, adding this to their Roster.

In a Team game all Posses involved Stake a Territory, and each Posse in the winning Team gets to choose a Territory Staked by an opposing Posse. Roll-Off to decide who gets first pick of the spoils!

If there are not enough Territories Staked by the losers, then the winners should just randomly generate a new Territory from the table.

If you lose your last Territory, you must immediately generate a new one at random.

The maximum Territories a Posse can control at one time is ten. If you would ever control more than this, you must choose Territories to discard until you have ten.

Worth

At the end of the Campaign (i.e. after the final Infamy calculations are made in the final Campaign Turn, but before an overall winner is determined) each Posse also gains bonus Infamy for the total Worth of all Territories they control, as follows:

Total Worth of Territories you control	Bonus Infamy at end of Campaign
0–5	0
6–10	1
11–15	2
16–20	3
21–25	4
26+	5

Territories with a random Worth (e.g. D6 for a Mine) roll to determine their value at this point and not before!

YOUR HIDEOUT

One (and only one!) Territory on your Roster must be chosen as your Posse's Hideout. If you lose your Hideout for any reason, it is destroyed and not kept by your opponent (if they took the Territory off you). You must then nominate a new Hideout if possible.

If you have no Territories, the next time you claim one it becomes your new Hideout automatically.

You may add Upgrades to your Hideout from the list below during any Purchase Phase. Each Upgrade can only be taken once per Hideout, and a Hideout can have a maximum of four Upgrades.

HIDEOUT UPGRADE TABLE		
Upgrade	**Cost**	**Notes**
Drinkin' Hole	$15	It may not be the most salubrious establishment in the world, but everyone likes a drink now and then! The maximum number of models allowed in your Posse becomes 12, rather than 10.
Gamblin' Den	$20	Fortunes (and lives) can be lost here, on the turn of a card... Once per Income Phase, you may gamble up to $10 from your Stash. Shuffle a deck of cards and reveal the top one. Now call 'Higher' or 'Lower' (Aces are high), draw and reveal the next card, and compare its value to the first — if you called correctly or drew an Ace, you double your money! If you called incorrectly or you drew a Joker, you lose your money.
Tradin' Post	$4	You'd be surprised at the kind of goods that find their way out here on the Frontier! If your Boss Searches for Uncommon Items in the Purchase Phase, they always find at least one.
Jailhouse	$20	Whatever side of the law you find yourself on, having a sturdy gaol in which to hold prisoners is a useful — and often lucrative — asset. Allows you to hold up to four Captured enemies and take Bounty Hunter Jobs between games (see page 67).
Sawbones	$8	If you're feeling poorly, a trip to the Docs will soon sort you out — if you survive the experience. You may visit the Doc with a single model suffering a Lasting Injury in each Injury Phase. Roll 1D6 — a 6 cancels that Injury, a 1 means the patient is Dead. Anything in-between has no effect.
Contacts	$12	Whether it's rich folks back East or shady dealers in back alleys, you always know who to go to get what you want and at the right price. Once per Purchase Phase, you may reduce the cost of a Weapon or other Item by $D3 (minimum $1).
Telegraph Office	$6	The wonders of modern technology makes reaching out across the Country a quick and (mostly) reliable process. You may re-roll the Die for determining your available Recruits during the Purchase Phase.
Local Rag	$12	When in doubt, always print the legend! Roll a D6 once per Infamy Phase — on a 1, lose one Infamy. On a 6, gain one Infamy. Anything in-between has no effect.
Storehouse	$20	A useful place to store your ill-gotten gains... Anytime a friendly non-Hired Gun model dies or leaves your Posse, you may add their Weapons and/or Gear to your Stash — it is not lost to you!

TERRITORY EVENTS

After the Advancement Phase, and immediately before resolving the Income Phase, each player with two or more Territories rolls 2D8. If any double is rolled, a Territory Event has occurred.

Look up the double rolled on the table below

TERRITORY EVENTS TABLE		
Double Rolled	**Event**	**Notes**
1	Natural Disaster!	Your Territories have been shattered by an Earthquake or Hurricane! Roll 1D6 per Territory you control. On a roll of 1 that Territory is removed from your Roster and replaced with a Badlands. If the Territory contains your Hideout, all Upgrades are lost, and you must choose another Territory from those remaining and start a new Hideout there.
2	Abandoned	Harsh conditions, restless Natives, and many other causes can lead to Territory being abandoned... Randomly select one Territory you control, not including Badlands or the Territory containing your Hideout. That Territory is removed from your Roster and replaced with a Badlands.
3	Raid!	Your enemies have launched a surprise attack on your base of operations — though you fight them off successfully, the damage may already have been done! Roll 1D6 for each Upgrade your Hideout possesses. On a 1 that Upgrade is removed from your Hideout.
4	Shortages	Whether it's due to a bad harvest, a worker's strike, or a lack of customers easily parted from their cash, times are lean in your Territories... When generating Income in the following Phase, you roll one less Die than normal. The effects of this Event last only until the end of this Campaign Turn!
5	March of Progress	Few can stand in the way of the relentless advance of the railroads... Randomly select one non-Railroad Territory you control, and replace it with a Railroad. If this Territory contains your Hideout, simply transfer it to the new Railroad.
6	Settlers	A fresh influx of hardy frontier-folk sees the population of your Territory explode. Randomly select one non-Town Territory you control, and replace it with a Town. If this Territory contains your Hideout, simply transfer it to the new Town.
7	Gold Rush!	There really is gold in them hills! Randomly select one non-Mine or non-Claim Territory you control, and replace it with a Claim. If this Territory contains your Hideout, simply transfer it to the new Claim.
8	New Frontier	Agents in your Territories have discovered a new area that is ripe for exploiting. Randomly generate a new Territory. If you already have 10 Territories, this Event has no effect.

Finding Animus

Much of the trouble currently consuming the Indian Territory can be attributed to that wondrous source of Arcane power known as Animus. Since Zeke Matheson's discovery of this miraculous new fundament, those wealthy dabblers in the Arcane Arts back East have been willing to pay almost any price for even the merest drop of Animus.

STRIKING IT LUCKY

During this Campaign the Posses are constantly on the look-out for points of Convergence that lead into the Hunting Grounds and, hopefully, a new 'seam' of raw Animus.

When rolling for Income, if you generate an Encounter you may also manage to gather one or more 'Portions' of Animus, which is added to your Stash before resolving the Encounter. The number of Portions found depends on whether you rolled two-, three-, four-, or even five-of-a-kind (always use the highest duplicate):

Multiple Rolled	Two-of-a-kind	Three-of-a-kind	Four-of-a-kind	Five-of-a-kind
Animus Portions	0	1	2	3

For example, Tony rolls for Income and scores 4, 4, 2, 2, 2. This generates $14 Income and a total of 1 Portion of Animus. He must then decide to resolve either the 'Aftermath' (double 4) or 'Wandering Medicine Man' (treble 2) Encounter.

Selling Animus

Animus can be sold in the Purchase Phase. However, the exact amount it is worth varies depending on how flooded the markets are back East, and how much of it accrues the new 'Animus tax' imposed by the Government! The tax can always be circumnavigated of course – but black marketeers have been known to take an equally large cut of a dealer's profits, so selling the stuff (whether legally or illegally) is always fraught with uncertainty…

To sell your Animus, first declare how many Portions you will sell, and mark them off your Roster. You can sell up to ten Portions in a single Purchase Phase.

You should then roll a D10 and multiply the score by the number of Portions you are selling – the total is the amount of Dollars added to your Stash.

OPPOSITE The Forsaken: The Accursed

Using Animus

Instead of selling Animus, you may decide to prepare it for use during a game. This is done immediately after resolving Encounters in the Income Phase – simply remove a Portion of Animus from your Roster and add one 'Vial of Animus' item (see page 42) in its place.

Any amount of Animus can be prepared in this way between games, and each Portion used makes one Vial.

Outlaws

Infamy can be a double-edged sword – the more notorious a Posse becomes, the more grudging respect and outright fear they create in their rivals – and the more everyone is out to take 'em down a peg or three!

Truly Infamous Posses become Outlaws – hunted men and women forced to eke out a meagre existence on the fringes of civilisation...

TROUBLE WITH THE LAW

After each game (but before starting the Injury Phase), the Posse with the highest current Infamy from amongst those who took part must roll a D10 and cross-reference the result on the table below. This is to see whether their nefarious deeds have seen them Outlawed. Where several Posses have equally high Infamy then they must Roll-Off, with the lowest scoring Posse rolling to see if they become Outlaw.

Outlaw Posses never roll on this table, even if they have the highest Infamy – the Posse with the next highest Infamy must roll instead!

OUTLAW TABLE						
	Die Score	1	2–3	4–7	8–9	10
	10 or less	Clear	Clear	Clear	Clear	Suspicion
	11–20	Clear	Clear	Clear	Suspicion	Suspicion
Infamy	21–30	Clear	Clear	Suspicion	Suspicion	Outlawed
	31–35	Clear	Suspicion	Suspicion	Outlawed	Outlawed
	36–40	Suspicion	Suspicion	Outlawed	Outlawed	Outlawed
	45+	Suspicion	Outlawed	Outlawed	Outlawed	Outlawed

Clear

The Posse is cleared of any wrong-doing, and there is no effect.

Suspicion

While no hard proof exists of the Posse's crimes, everyone knows they are up to no good and the Pinkertons are keeping a close eye on them!

Make a note on your Roster that your Posse is currently under Suspicion – the next time you roll on the Outlaw table above, you must treat your Infamy as being one bracket higher than it really is.

For example, my Posse's Infamy is currently 24 – I would therefore roll using the '21–30' bracket. However, I am under Suspicion so I roll using the 31-35 bracket instead!

If you ever roll a result of Clear while under Suspicion, then your Posse is no longer under Suspicion.

Suspicion is not cumulative, if you roll this result twice you remain under Suspicion but there is no further effect.

Outlawed

The Posse is run out of town and becomes Outlaw. Make a note on your Roster and refer to the following special rules.

OUTLAW POSSES

Life as an Outlaw may seem romantic and dashing, but in reality it is a harsh existence that more often than not ends very swiftly – and fatally!

On The Scout

Being Outlawed forces a Posse to keep on the run, hiding out in isolated areas, and staying away from civilisation for fear of being recognised. An Outlaw Posse is subject to the following rules:

- **Territory:** Outlaw Posses may never have more than 1 Territory. Any excess Territories (of your choice) are lost when you become Outlaw. If you win a game, you may swap the new Territory for your current one if you wish – any Hideout Upgrades on your current Territory will be lost for good, however...
- **Purchasing:** Outlaw Posses always roll a D6 on the Recruitment table regardless of their Boss' Grit. In addition, Outlaw Bosses deduct a further 1 from their roll when Searching for Uncommon Items.
- **Bounty:** The Bounty paid on Outlaw models is increased by 50%, rounded up.
- **Infamy:** In the Infamy Phase, an Outlaw Posse rolls a D6. On a 5+, their Infamy increases by 1 – in this way, the longer you are Wanted by the law the more fear and awe you inspire!

Blood Money

There is a way to cancel your Posse's Outlaw status – pay off the authorities with Blood Money!

This can be paid at the start of any Purchase Phase, before Recruitment occurs.

The Blood Money price is equal to your Posse's current total Infamy. As soon as you pay this amount, your Outlaw status is immediately lifted (until the next time you get into trouble!) and the above rules cease to apply.

It is entirely possible to pay your Blood Money, only to be Outlawed again shortly after if you are especially unlucky. Nobody said that running with a Posse would be easy!

OPPOSITE The Shadow Dragon Tong: Yanluo

BOUNTY HUNTING

During a game, a model that is Down can be Captured by an opposing model for its Bounty. NPCs and Bystanders cannot be Captured. You may only Capture models if your Posse's Hideout is upgraded with a Jailhouse.

Capturing Enemies

You Capture a Downed enemy model by moving into Contact with them. They then follow the rules for dragging comrades, except the captured model cannot be Activated and does not make Recovery Tests – instead, they simply remain Down.

If a Captured model no longer has an enemy in Contact with it, it is no longer a Captive and reverts to the usual rules for Downed models.

Calculating Bounties

A model's Bounty is equal to its personal Infamy multiplied by 3.

NPCs do not have Bounties.

Outlaw models are worth an additional 50% of this value, rounded up – see earlier for more on Outlaws.

For example, a Veteran with the Gunslinger and Mean Skills has a personal Infamy of 4. Its Bounty is therefore $12 (4 x 3). If their Posse was Outlawed, their Bounty would be $18 (12 + 6)!

The Rewards of Bounty Hunting

At the end of the game, a Captured model can either be turned over to the authorities by their Captor – in which case they count as Dead, and the Captor earns Dollars equal to their Bounty, or they can be kept in the Captor's Jailhouse and ransomed back to their own Posse (or otherwise traded for goods and/or favours) at a later date. It is up to the players to agree the exact terms of this exchange between themselves.

TAKING BOUNTY HUNTING JOBS BETWEEN GAMES

A single surviving non-Supernatural model in your Posse may take a Bounty Hunting Job between games if you wish. This is declared immediately after the Injury Phase – such models may take no part in the rest of this Campaign Phase. You may only take on Bounty Hunting Jobs if your Posse's Hideout is upgraded with a Jailhouse.

1: Determine the Job Difficulty

The first step is to determine the danger represented by the Job, by rolling a D6.

BOUNTY HUNTING JOB DIFFICULTY TABLE	
D6 Roll	Danger
1–3	Simple
4–5	Average
6	Dangerous

2: Determine any Complications

You must then determine if the Job has any complications – roll a D10:

BOUNTY HUNTING COMPLICATIONS TABLE		
D10 Roll	Outcome	Notes
1–5	No Complication	No effect
6	May The Best Hunter Win!	There is a rival Hunter pursuing your quarry. Before continuing, roll a D6 on their behalf on the Bounty Hunting table below to see how they do. If they complete the Job successfully, then they find the fugitive before you do and you get no Reward!
7	Bring Me His Head!	You will only earn a quarter of the Reward (rounding up) if you bring the fugitive back Alive.
8	I Want Him Alive and Unspoiled	You will earn no Reward if you bring the fugitive back Dead.
9	Just Protectin' My Investment...	Your employer insists on coming along. Roll a D6 if the Job succeeds – on a 1 they died during the Job and you get no Reward!
10	You Killed Mah Brother!	This fugitive is a relation of a previous quarry you brought in, and they are out for revenge! Increase this Job's Difficulty by 1. For example, 'Simple' becomes 'Average'. If this would take the Difficulty beyond 'Dangerous', apply a -2 modifier to your roll on the Bounty Hunting table instead of -1! However, if you succeed in this Job your notoriety grows and you receive +1 personal Infamy for this model.

At this point, you may decline the Job if you wish. The chosen Bounty Hunter may still not take part in the rest of this Campaign Phase.

3: Resolve The Job

If you decide to take the Job, you then roll 1 Grit Die on the Bounty Hunter's behalf.

Add 1 if the job is Simple. Deduct 1 if the job is Dangerous, unless your model is a Bounty Hunter Hired Gun.

Look up your final score on the table below:

	BOUNTY HUNTER JOB OUTCOME TABLE	
Score	**Outcome**	**Notes**
0 or less	Should've Stayed Home!	The Bounty Hunter is dead and their body is lost somewhere in the wilderness – remove them from your Roster
1	Bushwhacked	The Bounty Hunter is ambushed by the fugitive, and must make an Injury Roll. The Job ends in failure, regardless of the outcome of the Roll.
2–3	Elusive Prey	The Job ends in failure – the trail has gone cold!
4–5	Filled 'Em Fulla Lead	The fugitive is brought back Dead – you earn the appropriate amount.
6–7	Took 'Em Alive!	The fugitive is brought back Alive – you earn the appropriate amount.
8–9	Danger Money	The Bounty Hunter receives additional pay in light of the hardships they endured on this Job – roll a D6, and if the result is Odd the fugitive is brought back Dead. If Even, they are captured Alive. You earn the appropriate Reward, plus a further $D6 for a Simple Job, $D8 for an Average Job, or $D10 for a Dangerous Job.
10–11	This'll Make The Papers...	The fugitive (a notorious outlaw) is brought back Alive, after a long and dramatic chase – you earn the appropriate Reward. In addition, the Bounty Hunter model gains +1 personal Infamy and +D3 EXP!

OPPOSITE Hired Gun: Bounty hunter

4: The Payoff

If the Job is completed successfully, compare the difficulty of the Job and the Rank of the Bounty Hunter on the table below to determine the reward for bringing in the fugitive Dead or Alive.

Job Difficulty	Bounty Hunter Rank		
	Novice	Veteran	Hero
Simple			
Alive	$12	$8	$4
Dead	$6	$4	$2
Average			
Alive	$16	$12	$8
Dead	$8	$6	$4
Dangerous			
Alive	$20	$16	$12
Dead	$10	$8	$6

Mercenaries

It is not uncommon for experienced gunhands to do a little bit of moonlighting on the side during quiet periods – some successful Posses will even hire out their members as a lucrative (but dangerous) business venture!

HIRING MERCENARIES

You may hire out one of your non-Hired Gun Veteran or Hero Rank models to another Posse as a Mercenary if you wish and if the would-be Employer agrees.

However, some Factions will simply never work together no matter how much money is involved – the following Factions may never hire Mercenaries from each other:

- The Twilight Order and Red Hand Coven
- Skinwalker Tribes and The Crossroads Cult
- The Congregation and Dark Confederacy

Furthermore, a Mercenary will never fight against its own Faction and/or Posse for any reason!

Using Mercenaries

Once hired, the Mercenary counts as part of their Employer's Posse for all rules purposes for the next game, except where noted below, and can take no part in any other game this Campaign Phase.

After the game they will return to their own Posse, where they will earn EXP and otherwise take part in the rest of the Campaign Phase as normal (assuming they survive, of course!).

Mercenaries can never be the Boss of their Employer's Posse, regardless of relative Ranks.

They never add to the Infamy of their Employer's Posse.

A Posse that employed any Outlaw Mercenaries this Campaign Phase adds +1 to their roll to see if they themselves become Outlaws, should that be applicable!

A Mercenary usually falls under the control of their Employer. However, if the players agree then the owner of the model may control the Mercenary for the duration of the game. Remember that they still count as part of the Employer's Posse!

Mercenary Pay

The standard rate for a Mercenary (even an Outlaw) is $(3 x personal Infamy) + cost of Weapons/Gear. This is paid by the Employer to the Mercenary's parent Posse before the game in which they are to be used.

Players may of course make counter-offers (even mid-game, if everyone agrees to such skulduggery!), set their own rates, and even agree to compensation should their Mercenary die. This is all left to your group's discretion, but can be a lot of fun if played in the right spirit!

MERCENARY DRIFTERS

If you retire your Posse, or when your group reaches the end of a Campaign, you may decide to immortalise a single surviving model – not a Hired Gun or unique model (such as a Crusader of the Order) – as a Mercenary Drifter.

Each Posse may nominate a single model if their player wishes.

These hard-bitten survivors have seen the worst that Dracula's America can throw at them, and will surely have some tall (and terrifying!) tales to tell...

To qualify as a Drifter, a model **must**:

- Be of Veteran or Hero Rank
- Have at least one Skill

Copy the new Drifter's details onto a blank card (see page 92), including their Faction, Lasting Injuries, Weapons and Gear, and calculating their base hire fee of $(3 x personal Infamy) + cost of Weapons/Gear.

These cards can be kept to one side and perused by any prospective Employer – you may even use them from one Campaign to the next. In this way your gaming group will gradually build up its own unique rogue's gallery!

Recruiting a Mercenary Drifter

During the Recruitment segment of any Purchase Phase, you may send one model out to look for a single Drifter. This is achieved by rolling 1 Grit Die on behalf of the seeker, and on a score of 6 or better the Drifter has been found and agrees to join your Posse. At this point, you must pay their base hire fee. The Drifter will then become part of your Posse for the duration of the next game only, after which they will stride off into the sunset!

Where multiple Posses wish to hire the same Drifter, they should all roll to seek them. The highest successful roll gets to hire them. If this is still a tie, the deadlocked players must secretly write down a bid on a scrap of paper – this can be $0 if they wish. The competing bids are then revealed simultaneously, and the highest bidder may hire the Drifter. However, they must pay their stated bid in addition to the Drifter's base hire fee!

Mercenary Drifters will never Advance or roll for Injuries after a game like normal Mercenaries, they are semi-legendary figures who have achieved a kind of immortality and will reset back to the profile shown on their card after every game.

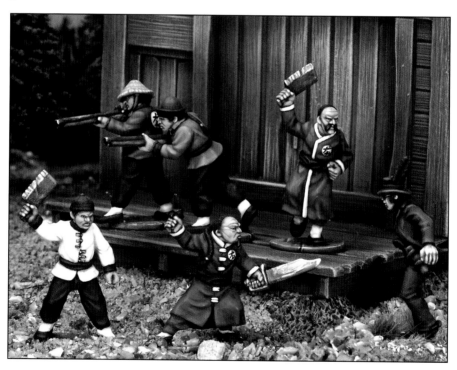

NARRATIVE CAMPAIGN

Playing a Narrative Campaign

If you are playing the Scenarios in this book as part of the larger ongoing narrative of Dracula's America, then the first thing you and your fellow players must do is decide your Posse's allegiance. Out here on the Frontier there is no sitting on the sidelines – your Posse must declare for one side or the other!

Alliance of Order

Posses of this Alliance are determined to uphold the status-quo in some form or another. This could mean keeping Dracula in power, retaining the Balance of the natural world, or simply fighting to protect the innocent from the various threats massing in the darkness...

Alliance of Chaos

Posses of this Alliance want nothing more than to see the world as it is come tumbling down in flames! They may want to create anarchy for the sheer joy of it, or seek to invite shadowy Entities into our reality – perhaps they are jaded agents of 'good' who believe the end always justifies the means?

As you can see, any Posse can belong to either Alliance with a little imagination. The reason can be as simple as a Posse being duped by its shadowy masters – unaware of the cause it is truly serving!

Wherever possible, your group should have a roughly equal number of players within each Alliance, though a bias of one or two players either way shouldn't be too much of an issue.

If you should find yourself with fewer players than you started with (because real life does have an unfortunate habit of getting in the way of the serious business of gaming!), then the group can vote for one or more Posses to switch allegiance (or somebody can just volunteer) and so retain the balance between the two. This is the only way you can change your Alliance during the Narrative Campaign, and you should come up with a suitably dramatic and/or entertaining reason for your Posse to turn traitor!

DESTINY POINTS

Each time you finish a Scenario from this book, you should make a note of which Alliance the winning Posse (if there is one) belongs to. That Alliance gains 1 Destiny Point.

If the game featured Posses from only a single Alliance, no Destiny Point is awarded!

As you play through each of the expansion books, you should keep a running total of each Alliance's Destiny Points – at the end of the final book, this will determine the ultimate fate of America and your chosen Faction... So, no pressure!

Hunting Ground Scenarios

In one-off games, you may decide to roll 1D8 on this table instead of the one from the *Dracula's America: Shadows of the West* rulebook to generate a random Scenario. Alternatively, you may play through them in ascending order (i.e. from 1 to 7) as the first part of the ongoing Narrative Campaign!

If you want to expand the scope of your Campaign even more, feel free to intersperse these Scenarios with ones from the *Dracula's America* rule book. For example, playing a 'Shootout', followed by 'The Ghost Town', and then perhaps a 'Fistful of Loot' before playing 'The Key'. Tell the story your way!

All of the following Scenarios use the rules for traversing the Hunting Grounds given in the second chapter of this book.

HUNTING GROUNDS SCENARIO TABLE	
D8 Roll/Number	**Scenario**
1	The Ghost Town. A spectral town has appeared in the area, and is rumoured to hide lost treasures.
2	The Key. The Posses must track down an elusive Spirit-Walker before their rivals do.
3	The Rescue. The Posses enact a daring rescue mission in the Hunting Grounds.
4	The Hunt for Custer. The Posses close in on Custer and must chase him between realms to claim his secrets for themselves.
5	Maximum Convergence. As the Hunting Grounds begin to leak through into the physical realm on an unprecedented scale, the Posses vie to control both worlds!
6	The 3:10 to Purgatory. A Supernatural Train is racing deep into the secret heart of the Hunting Grounds, carrying a terrible cargo — can it be stopped?
7	The Spirit-Syphon. With the supernatural energy of the Hunting Grounds being syphoned away by the Crossroads Cult in order to power a dangerous ritual, the opposing Posses must try to prevent this...
8	Player's Choice! The Posse with the lowest total Infamy decides which Scenario to play. Otherwise, Roll-Off to determine who gets to choose.

SCENARIO 1: GHOST TOWN

The Skinwalker Shaman known as White Raven has enacted a powerful ritual that has weakened the boundaries between our world and the spirit realm beyond.

This has awakened the 'Spirit-Walker's Gift' in a minority of hitherto unremarkable people, allowing them to perceive and interact with the Hunting Grounds.

However, there are side-effects of this mighty Medicine that even the far-sighted White Raven could not have foreseen...

For where the veil between worlds is weakest, the eerie terrain and hungry spirit-creatures of the Hunting Grounds are able to manifest – albeit for only short periods – in the physical realm.

One such instance of so-called Convergence has occurred in the local area, and now rumours of an ethereal 'ghost town' trapped halfway between our world and the next have begun to circulate around the bustling mining town of Deadwood on the borders of Indian Territory.

Of more interest to the rival Posses loitering in the saloons around town, are the stories of the ancient treasures said to be hidden within its ghostly bounds...

Set-Up

Set up the table as for a normal game – there should however be four buildings placed no further than 8" from the centre of the table. These represent the ghost town.

If you are using more buildings than this then you will need to mark the ghost town out in some way!

Within each building of the ghost town, place a Loot counter.

Special Rules

The ghost town (and the Loot it contains) starts the game in the Hunting Grounds.

Starting from Turn 2, at the start of each Turn roll a D6 for the ghost town, on a 4+ all the buildings will shift from the Hunting Grounds and into the physical realm or vice-versa; along with everything inside or on them!

Any model can pick up a Loot counter as long as the model is in the same realm as the counter.

OPPOSITE Spirit Creature: Angry Spirit

Winning

In addition to the usual VP scoring method, at the end of the game each Loot counter held by your Posse is worth 3 VP.

SCENARIO 2: THE KEY

As useful an advantage as using the Hunting Grounds for travel is, it is reliant upon identifying and maintaining your control of those locations where the walls between worlds are weakest.

This is by no means an exact science, and the Factions require a more reliable means of traversing the Hunting Grounds to truly take advantage.

In recent weeks, rumours have begun to arise concerning individuals possessing the Spirit-Walker's Gift, who are able to step between worlds at will. Having such useful talents at their disposal would really give your Posse the drop on their enemies!

Now, your weary days of loitering in the saloons of Deadwood City in search of more information have finally paid off. An old prospector, freshly returned from his claim, has been overheard telling tales of a lone figure wandering in the

Black Hills – a shaman with the ability to step between the realms as easily as a normal man might step through an open door.

You resolve to capture and secure this valuable asset at any cost – it's just a shame that your rivals are thinking exactly the same thing!

Set-Up

Before Deployment, place a single Spirit-Walker model in the centre of the table. The Posses then Deploy in the usual manner.

Special Rules

The Spirit-Walker uses all the rules for Innocent Bystanders, except that they cannot be Attacked or used as a human shield. When the Spirit-Walker would Activate (i.e. not if it is being held by another model), roll a D6 on its behalf:

- On a roll of 1-3 they Move exactly like a Bystander.
- On a roll of 4+ they will immediately Spirit-Walk to or from the Hunting Grounds – as applicable – and then immediately make a Move like a Bystander.

The Spirit-Walker will always try to Move away from the closest visible model that could interact with it. For example, they ignore all models in the physical realm for these purposes if they are in the Hunting Grounds.

Furthermore, they will never leave the table and will stop at the edge should their full movement take them off.

Finally, the Spirit-Walker is ignored by all NPCs.

Winning

In addition to the usual VP scoring method, at the end of the game the Posse holding the Spirit-Walker earns 6 VP.

SCENARIO 3: LOST IN THE HUNTING GROUNDS!

The Posses are loitering around Deadwood looking for trouble as usual, when the locals erupt into frenzied activity – it seems a party of explorers disappeared into a nearby point of Convergence, and have not been seen for several days!

Though this is nothing new in recent weeks, what has everybody so agitated is that amongst the lost party was a member of an incredibly wealthy family from back East (rumoured to be favourites of Dracula himself!). Their representatives arrived in town yesterday, and since then have been making rounds of all the saloons, making it known that they will pay a handsome reward to the individuals who brave the spirit realm and bring back the VIP.

Being braver (or more foolhardy) than most, the Posses have struck out for the last known location of the lost expedition, little realising that something ancient and malevolent is out hunting as well...

Set-Up

Before Deployment, place two Bystander models – plus one Bystander for each Posse taking part in the game – between 4" and 8" of the centre of the table. These models are Lost in the Hunting Grounds.

They are placed Down and with a Spirit Token to show they are in the Hunting Grounds.

Each player takes it in turns to place one Lost model at a time.

The Posses then Deploy using the normal rules for Deployment Zones.

Special Rules

The Lost models take no real part in the game – they do not make Recovery Tests and cannot be attacked.

Any model may Contact them and drag them as if they were a friendly model, as described in the main Rulebook. The first time a Lost model is Contacted, roll a D6 – on a 6, this model is also the VIP. If all other Lost models have already been Contacted or removed from play, the remaining Lost model is always the VIP!

When a model leaves the Hunting Grounds while in Contact with a Lost model, the Lost model is 'rescued' and immediately removed from play.

Starting from Turn 2 onwards, a terrifying Spirit Creature known as a Spirit-Eater may manifest in the Hunting Grounds, drawn by the scent of fresh prey! At the start of the Turn, roll a D6 – if the score is equal to or under the current Turn number, the Spirit-Eater appears in the centre of the table. See page 23 for its rules – however, it is also subject to the special rules given below.

The Spirit-Eater will Activate along with other NPCs but will always Move towards the closest visible Lost model (or in a random direction if this is not possible). If it Contacts a Lost model, that model's spirit is devoured and they are immediately removed from play! If there are no Lost models on the table at the start of any Turn, the Spirit-Eater immediately vanishes to hunt other prey, and is removed from play.

There can only ever be a single Spirit-Eater in play at one time during this Scenario – if it is Banished from play, roll to see if a new one manifests in the next Turn!

Winning

In addition to the usual VP scoring method, each Lost model you successfully rescue is worth 2VP. If this model is the VIP, you earn 4VP instead! If a model manages to Banish a Spirit-Eater from play, their Posse earns a further 2VP.

OPPOSITE Spirit Creature: Spirit Eater

SCENARIO 4: THE HUNT FOR CUSTER

Rumour has it that Custer and a handful of his men did not die at the Battle of Little Big Horn – Cursed by the Great Spirit for their outrages against the Native American peoples, their torn and bleeding bodies were in fact washed into the Little Big Horn River...

The Posses have discovered that the rumours now being whispered around the mining camps are true – Custer did indeed survive the Battle of the Little Big Horn – but he is not the man he once was.

The campfire horror stories hold that the erstwhile General is afflicted by a curse, that he and his surviving men take the form of monstrous beasts when angered, that they walk between worlds as instinctively as any Shaman, and that they make their lair somewhere deep in the shadowy realm of the Hunting Grounds...

If this is true, you must capture Custer alive and learn his secrets for yourself. However, it is unlikely he will come quietly!

Set-Up

Before Deployment, place a monstrous Skinwalker in Beast Form as close to the centre of the table as possible. This, believe it or not, is General Custer himself... And he's really riled!

You will also need a model to represent Custer in his much less terrifying Human Form.

Once this is done, Deploy your Posses in the usual way.

Special Rules

Custer is on a 40mm base, has Grit D10 and a Move of 6". He has the Bull-Rush and Fearsome Skills. In addition, he always gains a +2 Dice Modifier in a Fight.

Custer remains in Beast Form, and follows all the usual NPC rules. However, he does not suffer Damage in the usual way. Instead, he has 6 Hit Points. Each time he suffers a 'Shaken' result, he loses 1 Hit Point. Each time he suffers a 'Downed' result, he loses 2 Hit Points. Each time he suffers a 'Removed as a Casualty' result, he loses 3 Hit Points. Upon losing all his Hit Points, Custer is Downed.

Whenever he suffers any Damage that does not Down him, Custer will automatically Spirit-Walk into or out of the Hunting Grounds, depending on his current location.

Whilst Downed, he transforms into his Human Form and can be grabbed and dragged like a Bystander. However, he is too valuable to be attacked or used as a Human Shield!

Unless he is being held in the above manner, then at the end of the Recovery Phase he will automatically Recover and transform back into his Beast Form, but with only 2 Hit Points remaining.

Winning

In addition to the usual VP scoring method, at the end of the game, the Posse in possession of Custer earns 6VP.

SCENARIO 5: MAXIMUM CONVERGENCE

Custer has been captured by the Crossroads Cult.

Now, with the Forsaken's secrets revealed to him, Edward Crowley has found a way to pull at the Arcane threads that hold the fabric of the planes together – already weakened by White Raven's ritual, the barriers have begun to crumble and even collapse completely in places, allowing the two worlds to merge fully in certain areas. Needless to say, chaos has ensued!

Confused and angry Spirit Creatures have begun to assail frontier towns in ever-greater numbers, and entire wagon-trains have inadvertently wandered into the Hunting Grounds by mistake – their unprotected soul's easy prey for the hungry entities lurking within!

Somebody needs to step in and restore some order, before the Indian Territory is swallowed up by the Hunting Grounds once and for all...

Set-Up

Before Deployment, divide the table into equal quarters.

Place 1 Objective as close to the centre of each quarter as possible. These represent portals to the Hunting Grounds. Each Objective can be represented by a 40mm plastic miniatures base or other appropriate marker.

Two randomly-determined Objectives must also start the game with a Spirit Token – they are within the Hunting Grounds and can only be claimed by models there.

Special Rules

At the start of each Game Turn except the first, roll 1D6 for each Objective:

- On a 1–3, the Objective shifts into the other realm, so from the Hunting Grounds to the physical realm or vice-versa, gaining or losing a Spirit Token as appropriate.
- On a 4+, the Objective remains in its current location.

Winning

In addition to the usual VP scoring method, at the end of the game each Objective that has more of your models (Downed models do not count!) within 3" of it and in the same realm, is claimed by your Posse and scores 3 VP.

If an Objective has equal numbers of viable opposing models within 3" of it, it is contested and is worth

1 VP to each contesting Posse.

SCENARIO 6: THE 3:10 TO PURGATORY

This Scenario is ideally played with no more than two opposing forces – if you have three or more players you can form up into Teams.

Chaos consumes the Indian Territory – from Deadwood City to the Black Hills and beyond. The Hunting Grounds have begun to Converge with the physical plane to an unprecedented degree!

It is during this confusion, while his enemies are focused elsewhere, that the Grand Magister of the Crossroads Cult, Edward Crowley, has begun the final phase of his diabolical plan to exploit the Arcane energies that infuse the Hunting Grounds.

A new railroad now snakes its way across the plains but this one is forged of infernal iron and exists in two realms. The gossips in Deadwood speak of a 'phantom train' which hurtles through the night, driven by demons, and carrying off the souls of the unwary...

The truth is worse than the gossips could ever imagine (as is usually the case!). For this Train, and the others that run the line, are carrying Arcane cargo from our world deep into the Hunting Grounds.

From his new base-camp in Custer's old lair, Crowley is constructing a terrible, dark Spell that will consume the purest Animus found only at the very heart of the Hunting Grounds, and use it to empower his Great Ritual tenfold!

As the Posses converge on the location of one such Phantom Train, the speeding locomotive begins to flicker in and out of the physical realm before their very eyes.

It must be stopped before it can reach the Hunting Grounds, and Crowley's diabolical plans come one step closer to fruition...

Set-Up

Designate one table-edge as the Eastern Edge.

Running along the centre-line of the table, from the centre of the Eastern Edge to the centre of the Western Edge is the track. This should be between 2" and 3" wide.

Place the Train on the track, with its front in Contact with the centre of the Eastern Edge. Place the Engine first, and then 3 Carriages moving back towards the Western Edge.

Each half of the table (as delineated by the track) must have between 1 and 3 Terrain elements in it. Terrain cannot be placed on the track, inside any Deployment Zone, within 3" of the track, or any other Terrain element.

Each Posse can only take up to half its current number of models (to a minimum of 3, unless the Posse comprises 4 or less models to start with, in which case the owning player chooses how many models to use) in this Scenario. The owning player chooses who to bring to this Scenario.

Dark Confederacy Revenants can be used in addition to the allowed models – though you will need suitably undead horses for them to ride!

All models are assumed to be riding a standard Horse. In a Campaign, only models that already had a Horse before this Scenario may keep theirs after this Scenario!

Flying models, and models with a base Move rate of 6" or more, may be used but do not get a Horse. Wolf Skinwalkers will start the Scenario already in Beast Form!

Deploy your Posses out from the North West and South West corners in the usual way.

Special Rules

Events and Agendas are not used in this Scenario.

At the end of each Game Turn, all terrain elements are moved a full 8" straight back, directly away from the Eastern Edge. Start with the terrain pieces closest to the Western Edge, then proceed towards the Eastern Edge.

If any terrain piece moves 'into' a model, then they are pushed along with it in the direction of travel. A model that is pushed off the table in this way may not return but does not have to roll for Injury after the Game!

Terrain that is moved off the Western Edge is removed from the game but is then immediately recycled by placing it in Contact with the Eastern Edge following the rules given in Set-Up. Roll-Off to determine who gets to place this

OPPOSITE The Forsaken: General Custer

terrain – it cannot be placed so that it is in Contact with any model! It will be moved again as above in the next Game Turn.

Once all elements have been moved, and from Game Turn 3 onwards, roll a D6. On an Odd number the entire Train and everything aboard shifts either into or out of the spirit realm as applicable. On an Even number the Train remains in its current dimension!

Each time a model Moves, it travels a number of inches equal to the roll of a D6+2 – a natural roll of 1 means the model may not Move at all this Action. This represents the uncertain conditions, the horses tiring, etc.

All Shooting in this Scenario suffers a -1 Die Modifier due to the high-speeds involved. Horses may not be Targeted by any Attacks in this Scenario – all Attacks must Target the rider.

Models that are Downed are treated as a Casualty immediately if they are not on the train. Models aboard the train follow the usual rules for being Down.

A model may attempt to leap aboard the train as an Action if they are in Contact with it by Succeeding a 1 Die Reaction Test. Failure means that the Action is wasted. Failure on a 1 means the model is removed as a Casualty!

Success means the model is placed inside the train. Once inside, a model may spend 1 Action to climb up onto the roof. If your model train does not allow you to place figures inside, they will leap straight up onto the roof instead.

It is possible for a model to be Shoved off the roof in a Fight. If this happens, the unfortunate model is Removed as a Casualty immediately!

Any model on a 25mm base and that is aboard the Engine may Take Control as an Action if no enemy model is also currently on the Engine. This model may spend Move Actions to slow down the Train – each Action spent in this way moves the entire Train 8" straight back (measure from the rearmost carriage), away from the Eastern Edge. If a model is Contacted by the Train during this movement, it becomes a Casualty immediately.

If a model gets the Engine off the Western Edge in this way, then their Posse wins the Scenario immediately.

Winning

Unless a Posse gets the Engine off the Western Edge as noted above, the Posse with the most models within 3" of the Engine and in the same dimension at the end of the game is declared the winner. Models actually aboard the Engine count as two models for this purpose, unless Downed, these models do not count at all!

SCENARIO 7: THE SPIRIT-SYPHON

Despite the best efforts of his rivals, one of Crowley's Phantom Trains has reached the very heart of the Hunting Grounds, carrying its Arcane payload with it.

The resulting shockwave of supernatural energies has been felt in both realms, and yet more dimensional walls have come crashing down! Those already within the spirit realm now feel a strange pull on their souls, as if being drawn elsewhere against their will...

They are being drawn towards the dark Heart of the Hunting Grounds, where there now stands a monstrous column of writhing shadow, turning lazily in place like some unnatural tornado with flashes of crimson lightning flickering at its core.

This is the culmination of Crowley's plans for the spirit realm. A huge 'Spirit-Syphon' that is designed to channel the raw ethereal energies of the place and feed them into the Crossroad Cult's own Great Ritual – empowering its dark magic tenfold

White Raven, horrified at the threat he has unwittingly unleashed, has sent his most trusted warriors (and some unlikely allies) into the Hunting Grounds in a desperate attempt to disrupt the spell binding the Syphon before the spirit realm is drained of all energy and the cosmic balance is irrevocably damaged!

Yet even as these defenders of Order lay eyes on the Syphon, they become aware of dark shapes forming within the eye of the magical storm – Abyssal Entities feeding off the raw power generated from the plundered essence of the Hunting Grounds, as the chains binding them in their infernal prison begin to loosen and then crack!

Opposing them stand the fanatical, hooded ranks of the Cult chanting the forbidden words that will maintain the spell's integrity. Around them stand those deluded men and women who have thrown in their lot with Chaos, their weapons held ready to defend their new allies.

This is it – the final showdown!

Set-Up

Before Deployment, place a large circular marker roughly 5" in diameter (an old CD or DVD painted appropriately is ideal) in the centre of the table, this is the Spirit-Syphon.

The usual Deployment rules are then followed.

Special Rules

No Posse takes Bottle Checks in this Scenario – this is the deciding battle for domination of the Hunting Grounds – and everyone must fight to the last.

The Spirit-Syphon blocks LOS between models either side of it, and provides Cover to models wholly within it.

It is completely impassable to Spirit Creatures (i.e. one from the Bestiary in this book) and Totem Spirits (Wolf, Bear, and Horse).

Any other model touching the Syphon in the physical realm at the end of any Move may choose to end that Action in the Hunting Grounds, or vice-versa. Give the model a Spirit Token as appropriate.

In addition, any Arcanist in Contact with the Syphon will always gain the effects of a Vial of Animus item (see page 42) when making Casting Tests.

Finally, beginning from Game Turn 4, at the start of each Turn one player (it doesn't matter who) must roll a D6 to see if an Abyssal Entity tears its way into the physical realm (the rules for which can be found on page 16):

ABYSSAL ENITITY TABLE	
D6 Roll	**Effect**
1–3	Nothing Happens
4	Hell-Hound
5	Fiend
6	Behemoth

These creatures are placed in the centre of the Syphon, and in the physical realm. They follow the usual rules for NPCs.

Winning

At the end of the game, each Posse scores 1VP for each of its models that is within 3" of the Syphon, or 2VP for each of its models in Contact with it. Downed models do not count!

There is no other way to score VP in this Scenario, so Agendas are not used.

The Posse with the most VPs wins.

If played as part of the Narrative Campaign, then the Alliance with the most models in Contact with the Syphon (across all aligned Posses) at the end of the game earns an extra Destiny Point regardless of who actually won!

Campaign Aftermath

If you want to preserve the mystery of our ongoing tale, then do not read any further until you have played through the entire Hunting Grounds Campaign!

Total up which Alliance currently has the most Destiny Points, and look up their entry – and **only** that entry – page 93 for the Alliance of Order, page 94 for the Alliance of Chaos.

If both Alliances are tied, treat it as a victory for Order.

CAMPAIGN ROSTERS

Campaign Territory Roster

Posse Name	
Faction	
Hideout Type	
Hideout Upgrade	**Notes**
Territory Type	**Worth**

Mercenary Drifter Cards

MERCENARY DRIFTER	Name	Faction	Base Hire Fee	Rank/Grit
	Skills			
	Weapons			
	Gear			
	Injuries			

MERCENARY DRIFTER	Name	Faction	Base Hire Fee	Rank/Grit
	Skills			
	Weapons			
	Gear			
	Injuries			

MERCENARY DRIFTER	Name	Faction	Base Hire Fee	Rank/Grit
	Skills			
	Weapons			
	Gear			
	Injuries			

Campaign Aftermath: Alliance of Order

Crowley's plans have been confounded once again by the Alliance of Order.

However, as the Spirit-Syphon imploded, a shockwave of Arcane power erupted forth and shook the very walls of reality. Already weakened mystical barriers shattered throughout the Hunting Grounds, and a tide of Abyssal creatures flooded in through the gaps.

It took several weeks of desperate fighting to stem this tide of evil – during which an unlikely alliance between Dracula's troops, White Raven's Skinwalkers, and Crusaders of the Twilight Order fought against and defeated an Abyssal horde in the so-called Battle of Deadwood. It was discovered that the Abyssals were not seeking to conquer the material realm as originally feared but rather, they were desperately attempting to escape something far, far worse that at first seemed content to lurk out in the farthest reaches of the Void. Something incalculably ancient and alien to even the denizens of the Abyssal Plane... Something hungry...

It was not long before Arcanists and Animus-addicts throughout the world began to suffer from terrible nightmares in which tentacles of shadow writhed and a multitude of alien eyes glared from the darkness of twisted dimensions beyond time and space. Doomsayers and apocalyptic cults sprang up seemingly overnight as a wave of madness and insanity began to grip those sensitive to such things. Within the space of just a few months, many asylums across America were at full capacity.

The Alliance of Order desperately sought the source of this so-called Plague of Madness, and eventually found it to be emanating from deep within the bayous and swamps of the Deep South.

Braving the cursed undead of the Dark Confederacy, their agents discovered that many previously submerged ruins of cyclopean architecture had recently forced their way from the murk to the surface, and it was from these alien, weed-choked structures that the foul Plague of Madness was being emitted.

A new threat, born from Crowley's meddling with the fabric of reality, was rising in the South...

Campaign Aftermath: Alliance of Chaos

The Indian Territory situation has spiralled out of control and the Alliance of Chaos could not be more pleased!

With the Alliance of Order defeated, the Cult's Spirit-Syphon quickly reached full strength and sent a surge of unfettered Arcane power pulsing through Crowley's network of railroads, gradually eroding the already-weakened dimensional walls of the Hunting Grounds until, like the tide crashing into shore, the hordes of the Abyss flooded in. Across the Territory, the Physical, Spirit and Abyssal planes merged and twisted together into a nightmare realm where the Natural Balance collapsed completely; a taste of the full chaos that Crowley intended to unleash upon the world...

This glorious anarchy lasted for several weeks, until even Deadwood City itself seemed to writhe like a wounded beast and hellish creatures roamed at will in the streets and alleys. Even the mysterious Shadow-Dragon Tong melted away into the shadows in the face of this terror.

Forewarned weeks before by Pinkerton Agents within the city, Dracula sent his troops to try to contain the situation in Deadwood and salvage what he could of the lucrative Animus Trade. For a brief time vampiric creatures and US Army soldiers fought alongside Crusaders of the Order and ferocious Skinwalkers against Abyssal monsters and fanatical cultists, in what became known as the Battle of Deadwood.

Though the situation in Deadwood was stabilised – albeit tenuously – by this unusual alliance of erstwhile enemies, the forces of Chaos looked on with glee at the mayhem they had wrought.

And then something changed – something that even they could not have foreseen in their most deranged nightmares...

The Abyssal hordes began to leave the physical realm, abruptly abandoning their foothold in the mortal plane.

At the same time, Arcanists and Animus-addicts throughout the world began to report terrible nightmares in which tentacles of shadow writhed, and a multitude of alien eyes glared from the darkness of twisted dimensions beyond time and space.

A wave of insanity known as the Plague of Madness began to grip those sensitive to such things, and in the sudden silence following the departure of the Abyssal creatures the nation seemed to hold its breath, as if awaiting some new calamity that it instinctively knew was coming...

In the Deep South it was discovered that many previously unknown, submerged ruins of cyclopean architecture had recently forced their way out of the murk in the dark heart of the bayou, and it was from these alien, weed-choked structures that the madness was insidiously spreading across America.

Whatever happens next, the Alliance of Chaos stands ready to capitalise on the ensuing anarchy...

DRACULA'S AMERICA

SHADOWS OF THE WEST

FORBIDDEN POWER

COMING JULY 2018

Since Dracula's rise to power a shadow has swept across the nation, but nowhere is it darker than in the Deep South. Throughout the plantations, swamps, and cities, rumours abound of grotesque rituals, hooded figures, and bizarre creatures. Most terrifying of all, however, are the whispers of ancient magic – unspeakable arcane rituals and occult powers that can lead those who wield them towards mystical supremacy… or reduce them to gibbering wrecks.

This new supplement for *Dracula's America: Shadows of the West* introduces two new factions: the corrupt cultists of the Church of Dagon and the Salem Sisterhood, occult practitioners whose history dates back to the early Colonies. New stealth rules allow for all manner of sneaky and underhanded tactics, while expanded rules for arcane powers offer glory but could cost you your sanity. Alongside these are a host of new scenarios, Hired Guns, monsters, skills, and gear to challenge or assist those who dare venture into the Deep South of Dracula's America.